THE MAN WITH THE

GREEN SUITCASE

A Novel

By Dee Doanes

The Man With the Green Suitcase Copyright © 2012 by Dee Doanes
First Edition

ISBN: 978-0-615-67508-4

Cover Design: Roy Migabon

To my mother. I love you so much. To all the great writers of the world.

"When asked why I write, I say it is why I breathe. How I make my heart beat with life. It must be done so I can exist."
Dee Doanes

ACKNOWLEDGMENTS

Many thanks to Ann Kempner Fisher, my Fairy
Godmother Editor and good friend.
You're the best editor, teacher and motivator.

Special thanks for the loving guidance of my
Muse, K.M.

DO YOU SEE HIM?

Do you see him? Do you see him?
There he is walking down the street
on trembling legs, with a green suitcase.

I wonder what's inside.
I wonder where he is going.

He's not walking fast. He's not walking
slow.
He's just walking. Just walking.

Look at his face, a map of places he's
been.
It tells of the journey to Hell and back.

Each gray in his hair has a story all its
own,
of children that died and loves that were
lost.

He's not walking fast. He's not walking
slow.
He's just walking. Just walking.

His face filled with sweat. His eyes filled
with fire.
He's waiting to be reborn.

Until then, he's just walking. Just
walking.
Not walking fast, not walking slow.

Just walking. Just walking.

Chapter 1
THE MAN

Peachtree Street in the Buckhead section of Atlanta is a great place to people watch; the stylish socialites and well-heeled businessmen fill the sidewalks. It's the mini Beverly Hills of the South with its expensive boutiques and chic restaurants on every corner. Giacomo's restaurant is one such place and this night it's filled with the usual crowd of beautiful people. Fingers are swirling forks of delicately prepared Lasagna Matta, while Barolo wine is being sipped enthusiastically. Silk wrap dresses and two-piece suits clad the hungry diners. The maitre d' tells a walk-in couple that they can't be seated since they have no reservations. The unlucky couple leaves and waits for the valet to bring their car. As they get into their car and drive off, the valet goes to the front of the alley behind Giacomo's to steal a quick smoke. Further down the alley near a dumpster are empty boxes of Pellegrino water, Barolo wine, and tomatoes. Next to the dumpster crates are stacked against the wall like a pyramid. This is *not a* fine place to be for an old, disheveled man wearing a soiled green jacket, torn white shirt, holey dark blue pants, and dirty high top white tennis shoes, sitting on top of this throne of crates. His finger is poking in an empty can of crushed tomatoes. His stomach grumbles in discontent. He tosses the can to the side and with a deep sigh says aloud, "A fancy place like this should only use fresh tomatoes."

The man climbs down, bones popping and creaking a little, and leans against the building, eyes closed. His eyes open and he moves the boxes and unzips his pants. He crouches, winces as he fingers a thick scar on the side of his hip. His legs tremble a little and he leans against the building for support. "Uhhn." He strains to relieve himself.

A door to his left slams and some people walk out. A female voice says, "Tony, we need to make sure we have enough staff for the Bradley private party on Wednesday."

"Jeremy has that covered. You just need to confirm the final head count," the brisk voice of Tony Vitrelli, the owner of Giacomo's, replies.

That voice sounded like authority, like the manager or something, thought the man. As they continue talking the old man squeezes his butt tight to not attract attention. Plop! Too late, some hits the side of the can he had thrown away, and it rolls in the direction of the voices.

Conversation pauses as footsteps come to within a few feet of the man.

Tony yells angrily, "Get the hell out of here, you bum! Go take a dump on another block."

The woman frowns, giving Tony a disapproving look. The old man quickly pulls up his pants, crouching with his back to them. Quietly he says, "I'm sorry. I thought no one would be back here."

"Get going before I call the cops! And don't ever come back again."

Tony takes a few more steps toward the man, squinting to see him in the dark as the man rises from the side of the boxes and turns toward him. There is a hint of dignity in his upright stance as he steps into the street light. Criss-crossed all over his face are so many deep wrinkles they look like lines on a state map. Tony's stare meet with the hazel eyes of one not so old, yet his face is very old. Tony's eyes widen with surprise and confusion and his jaw drops, mesmerized and a little scared at the same time. The man's wrinkles are pulsating and seem to stretch out and curve at the edges. There is faint sound of rushing water as the wrinkles move. The old man steps toward the crates and motions as if he is going to climb on top, but instead, reaches up to a crate next to the top crate, and picks up a frayed, old green leather suitcase. The street light flickers and the man's face once again has the normal drooping lines one would see on any old face. Tony blinks rapidly for few seconds, thinking it was a trick of the light. The man turns and walks away. "Have a good night," he says.

The green suitcase is swinging slightly in his hand. It looks circa 1950's, leather peeling, but sturdy, with pieces of red and white fabric poking out. Tony watches until he can no longer hear the footsteps retreating into the far end of the alley.

Chapter 2
ON THE RUN

Just before sunrise, the old man cuts across the Carter Center, through the apartments on the right side to get to Ponce de Leon Avenue more quickly. He stretches his tall frame, yawns and runs crooked fingers through his thick nest of dark and gray hair, then brushes dirt off his dingy clothes. After a night of sleeping on the grassy area in front of the #6 bus stop, his hunger hasn't abated. He sucks his teeth thoughtfully, tasting the enamel, but that does nothing for the gurgling in his belly. But everything will be okay...it always is. Thirsty, he stoops to pick blades of grass that can quench the thirst a little if you suck them before the hot sun's rays takes the dewy moistness back into the sky. A sparkle in the grass catches his attention. He walks toward a little patch of grass near an old pipe next to the sewer and sees a silver and diamond wedding ring. He notices money stuffed inside the pipe and pulls it out to find several twenty-dollar bills. To the side of the pipe is a Blackberry cell phone still in the AT&T box. He nods, eyes wide, quickly snatching up everything and stuffing it into his green suitcase. The man takes off running for a few blocks, constantly looking over his shoulder to make sure no one is following him, clutching the suitcase close to his chest. He slows down to a fast walk for several more blocks, breathing heavily. A cop car drives by slowly. Damn, he doesn't want them to see him. The man ducks behind a tree, peeking around the corner to see if the coast is clear. He runs to the fence at the corner, quickly opens his suitcase and dumps the stolen items on the sidewalk just as a cop car pulls up to the fence.

"Hey, what're you doing?" the cop asks, leaning out of the window and looking curiously at the stuff on the ground.

The man quickly shuts his suitcase and runs, breathlessly saying over his shoulder, "I found that stuff near the apartments. Figured someone stole em'."

The cop begins to pull into the fenced back entrance of City Hall East police station, where all the cops gas up their cars.

"Hey, wait a minute, wait a minute! I want to ask you a few questions." Too late. Surprisingly, the old man picks up speed like an Olympic sprinter, ducks behind a house and runs in the opposite direction, going away from Ponce de Leon toward the back of a windshield repair shop on Glen Iris. They wouldn't know which direction he ran. Good, since he didn't like talking to people anyway. He had privacy to maintain.

Chapter 3
TIME TO SEE

After a few hours of walking around and looking for things in trash cans and dumpsters outside various shopping centers, the man with the green suitcase arrives at a house he hadn't been to in a while. They passed out tickets for turkey and cheese sandwiches. If he was lucky, maybe he could get on the list for a shower and a change of clothes too, which normally happens on Wednesday. But the old man isn't sure what day it is since he has no watch and lost his pocket calendar.

He heads for the courtyard to wait until it's time to eat. The old brick house is already filled with men and women, all there for food and clothing. He goes to the corner on the far side of the house, away from the water spout where people lined up to wash their hands or drink from when the kitchen is closed or it isn't shower day. He likes to have quiet, which is hard to do when on the move in the street, and that corner is what is needed. He sits on the ground, loosens his shoes and massages his sore, cracked feet. The man smiles as savory smells from the kitchen drift in his direction.

"Hey, I haven't seen you in a while. How have you been, man?" a voice asks. The old man looks up and smiles.

"Hi, Eddie, I'm making it. How've you been?"

Eddie sits down next to him, removing a large backpack that looks too big for his scrawny frame. Though the old man was like a single cactus on the side of a desert road, occasionally he liked being watered by Eddie's company. Eddie was an unemployed construction worker who had fallen on hard times. He wasn't too nosy about the old man's business and told him about clean-up jobs for construction and paint projects to make a few extra bucks.

"I'm doing okay," Eddie replies. "Checking out some job leads. I need a cell phone though to get calls. Trying to see what I can sell to buy a cheap used phone." Eddie takes a washcloth from his backpack to wipe the sweat from his sunburned face.

"Man, you look like the devil's breath scorched you," the old man says. They both laugh. The old man opens his green suitcase, rummaging inside for a few minutes, then tosses Eddie a small bottle of sunscreen lotion.

Two big men walk into the courtyard. "Oh boy, here comes trouble times two,"

Eddie says in a low voice. He nods slightly in their direction. They're imposing figures: tall, as big as wrestlers, long ZZ Top-looking beards, and both have identical bushy thick eyebrows and dark eyes.

The old man watches them standing in the water spout line. "Oh, those twins. They look scary, like something pissed them off. What have they done?" he asks Eddie while eyeing the matching scowls on the faces of the men.

"They're not twins, just brothers, a year apart," Eddie explains. "I hear the cops are looking for the one with the pineapple tattoo on his arm, for a murder over in Dekalb County." He pauses for a second. "They're mad because they broke into a place near the Carter Center and stashed what they got, but someone stole it from their hiding spot."

The old man raises his eyebrows in surprise, then quickly looks away from them. Eddie looks at him anxiously. He didn't figure the old man was a thief. "What do you know about this? I hope you aren't involved 'cause those brothers aren't ones to mess with," he says in a worried voice.

The old man looks at Eddie. "I didn't steal anything." Eddie stares at him, sensing more wasn't being said. He curiously gazes at the brothers who were now washing their hands under the water spout.

Later, they head into the house to eat. A "welcome home" sign hangs on the doorknob. The house is much bigger inside than it appears from the outside. Several wooden benches and folding chairs line the yellow foyer that leads into the dining room. It's bright and cheery, filled with sunlight coming from several white circular windows. As they pass through the doorway, the old man notices a flyer announcing the death of Susan Dyer, the Catholic church volunteer who had run the Open Door Community House for 24 years. She had worked in several homeless shelters for most of her adult life. She had been a good woman. Looking at her smiling picture, the old man remembers her kind words and warm brown eyes. He wonders who would take over the house now that she's gone. He gets his answer soon after he sits down with a plate of food: a turkey sandwich, apple, chocolate pudding, and iced sweet tea. A short, rosy-cheeked woman with curly brown hair comes to the front of the dining room. She clears her throat and adjusts her glasses before saying, "Excuse me everyone, I don't mean to interrupt your meal, but I would like to introduce myself. My name is Leslie Harper, but folks call me Lee. I'll be running Open Door from now on. I know that Susan will be greatly missed and I will keep up her good work by being there for each of you. If there is anything I can do to assist you, please don't hesitate to ask." She smiles, then walks around to each table to talk to people. The old man starts fidgeting nervously and looking around, before wolfing down his sandwich and leaving the table quickly clutching the green suitcase. Lee stops at the table before the old man can get away. Eddie and Lee look puzzled as the old man runs off. Eddie opens his mouth to ask what was going on, but says nothing, figuring he will come back later.

Lee extends her hand to Eddie. "Hi, what's your name? I'm so happy to have you here. Are you doing okay?" Eddie smiles as he shakes her hand.

"I'm Eddie. Doing pretty good. I got a lead for a construction job. It's hard for me to apply since I don't have a phone. But I'll work it out."

Lee nods sympathetically. "I'll see if one of the volunteers has a cell phone and doesn't mind taking messages from the job for you. Just stop by the office before you leave."

"That's so nice of you," Eddie says. "Thanks." Lee walks off to finish meeting everyone in the dining room, then looking down at a clipboard list, counts the people in the dining room, looks down at the list again and counts one more time. One name is missing from the list. She looks around for the old man, doesn't see him, shrugs and then leaves. Eddie, too, looks around for the man, doesn't see him, and finishes his meal alone.

Lee heads to her office and sees the man with the green suitcase walking down the outside steps. She turns and walks in his direction. "Hi, how are you? I missed you in the dining room. What is your na—"

"Hi, Miss Lee, don't mean to be rude, but I'm in a hurry," he mumbles, cutting her off and walking faster.

"I don't mean to bother you," Lee says as she looks down at her clipboard again. "But, do you mind coming into my office for just a few minutes?" He stops, turns to look at her, then looks down at the ground like he is listening, waiting for something. Then he looks at her again, hesitating. The empty space is waiting for words to fill it. Lee stands next to him, smiling and adjusting her glasses. "I promise I won't hold you up." He sighs and goes back up the steps. Lee is close behind.

Once inside Lee's office she closes the door. The old man looks around. Yellow daffodils sit on a gray desk in the corner of the room. Pictures of the Virgin Mary and Jesus adorn the walls. The old man begins fidgeting nervously again. He looks at Lee and can feel something happening. There is a tingling in his hands and chest. Lee looks down at the clipboard. "I didn't get a chance to talk to you, and I noticed that your name wasn't on the—" Her mouth opens wide in surprise as she looks at the old man's face. His wrinkles have started to pulsate.

"No, no," he mutters. He closes his eyes, rubs his head, concentrating, then shakes his head as if bees are buzzing around his face. The old man tries to will it away. It is futile because he has no control over it. He hates when it happens like this. He suddenly stops and stands very still, then walks closer to Lee. She is motionless, frightened, clipboard clutched tight to her chest, and holding her breath. The wrinkles pulsate faster. The man reaches out his hand. "Don't be scared, Miss Lee. It's okay. Really it is. There is just something I have to...I must show. I don't know what it is until it comes out of me. But...this...this power shows itself where it wants to and where it's needed." He looks deeply into her eyes. Lee sees the truth in his eyes, knows instantly his words are real, even though she's scared. She becomes still inside her heart and soul and knows that it's okay. That he's okay.

"I just need you to touch my face, touch to find out what you need to know," the old man says. As Lee looks at the wrinkles she feels the energy reach out, vibrating toward her. She reaches her hand out slowly. The energy is beckoning her closer. Lee becomes more hypnotized by the pulsating wrinkles. The closer she gets she's no longer afraid. Lee wants to touch the writhing wrinkles. She hears rushing water—it reminds her of the time she went white-water rafting. Fish swimming downstream and wet rocks come to mind. Then, the images of rain pelting hard on the windows in her sunroom. The tips of her fingers are almost touching, almost touching his cheek. She thinks how much she used to like reading her prayer book in the little sunroom, with the sun streaming across her cheek. Why is she thinking about that? Hadn't thought about that in years. Lee touches the wrinkles on his left cheek. That part of his cheek immediately sinks in, like she had touched a secret panel and something would pop out. Lee is floating, yet she can feel her feet still on the floor of the office. Energy envelopes her body like a blanket. Tiny flickers of warmth are tickling her all over. She feels very peaceful. The old man's eyes are closed; he, too, looks peaceful. He's in a deep sleep with hands folded across his chest. His wrinkles get warmer and warmer until they get too hot to touch. The energy is pushing Lee back. Reluctantly her hand leaves his face and she rubs her hand, embracing the energy.

She steps back and sees a circle of white and yellow light has formed around the man, burning red in the center. Lee can hear a garbled voice and see the blurry shape of a woman as the redness slowly dissipates. "Coming back, coming back now," a soothing, vaguely female voice says. There is laughter in the distance. Lee sees the back of a woman running in the shelter's courtyard toward the front door. The woman turns briefly then turns her back again. She would recognize that quick flash of crooked, dimpled smile anywhere—it was her daughter Casey's smile. Now the laughter is louder, clearer. With it's up up, high in the sky note that ebbed into a deep chest

*chuckle—that was her laugh, too. Then
the scene turns red again, then clear. Lee
sees herself in the sunroom, crying, the
prayer book falling to the floor. "Had to
leave, had to leave. Will come back but
have a long journey afterward. So, don't
you worry, Leslie, don't worry, Lee." This
voice sounds like her own but is coming
from another place deep inside that has
never been touched, yet the voice is her
voice.*

The circle of energy goes away and the
old man's eyes open. They stare at each
other for a few minutes before the tears
slide down her face. Lee had not been in
the sunroom in five years, not since
Casey left. That prayer book still was on
the floor. She couldn't bear to go in that
room again or pick up the book since
that was the place her daughter was last
seen. But she was coming back. Lee had
tucked the sunroom memory away like
old clothes stuffed in a chest in the attic.
Lee had given up hope even though her
lips trembled with plaintive prayers to
God that she thought would never be
answered. But her daughter would be
coming home now.

"Thank you, thank you," Lee cries,
dropping to her knees at the man's feet.
"Bless you." The old man looks down at

her. He's embarrassed and uncomfortable.

"Don't thank me, it was your vision. Something it was time for you to know." He hesitates, then walks to the door. "Don't mention this to anyone. This was meant only for you." She nods, understanding. He leaves. Lee knows everything will be fine.

Chapter 4
GERALD

Having a vision is a good thing. It gives you direction. A purpose. It can change your life dramatically if you decide to make changes. Gerald Foley has a vision of doing great things in the restaurant business. Not that he isn't already very successful, but just like every entrepreneur, ambition is intravenously fed by desire into the veins 24 hours a day, 7 days a week. And Gerald is a consummate workaholic. He's worked hard for the last ten years building his commercial property business into a successful enterprise by developing and leasing upscale properties in prime locations in Atlanta, mainly midtown and Buckhead. Bad economy or not, Gerald doesn't like major changes but needs to expand outside his field of expertise to continue making a great deal of money. Soon, Gerald will be closing a huge multi-million dollar restaurant deal with his business partner, Tony.

Gerald enjoys looking the part of the high achieving man. He looks the same as his professional picture in his glossy company brochure—a nice looking, clean-cut businessman. This morning after spending extra workout time at the gym, while reading the Wall Street Journal, he tugs at the now smaller love handles that he had begun to diet away. He figures it will take one more month for them to be completely gone. Gerald changes into his usual polo shirt and khaki pants to run out the door and start the beginning of a 12-hour work day.

Gerald drives to Buckhead. At a stoplight he eyes a silver Jaguar at the car dealership that he's thinking of buying. He calls the property manager of the high rise building he owns. Most of the tenants are high powered law firms and technology companies.

"I'm on my way to pick up the tenant checks. I'll be there in a few minutes," he tells the manager.

On Peachtree Street, Gerald arrives at a sleek, black building. The lawn is neatly manicured and a large water fountain sits outside. He goes inside, picks up the checks from his property manager and leaves.

Gerald drives to the other side of town for his next appointment. He passes an old abandoned building on Martin Luther King Jr. Drive, covered in red and blue graffiti. Two men are in front, sitting on stacked up milk carts smoking cigarettes. He pulls into the driveway of the strip shopping center he owns and parks his Mercedes in front of a crooked, green sign that says, "Car Title Pawn and Check Cashing." The other shops in the center are a laundromat, rib joint, beauty supply store, African hair braiding place, and a vacant shoe repair shop. None of his business associates know that Gerald owns four other strip shopping centers just like this one, in poor neighborhoods. It's where he got his start in commercial real estate before expanding into Atlanta's upscale areas.

Gerald goes into his property manager's office, picks up tenant rent checks and leaves. He walks out at the same time an elderly black woman with long, silver hair comes out of the laundromat carrying a basket overflowing with clothes.

The old woman looks at Gerald, does a double-take and drops the basket. Shirts and panties drop and puddle around her feet on the ground. "You killed my husband!" she screams.

Gerald turns around and stares at her, then looks behind him.

She pushes her thick bifocal glasses onto her nose and screams louder, "I'm talking to you!"

People inside the shops come out, curious to see what's going on.

Gerald is surprised but manages to say, "You're mistaken."

The old woman slowly walks to Gerald clutching blue socks in one hand. She stops in front of him and angrily shakes the socks in his face. "There's no mistake. You killed my Henry."

She scowls furiously at Gerald. He calmly says, "I don't know him."

"Course you don't. He was nobody to you. You bled him dry. He used to own the shoe repair place here." The old woman points her gnarled finger in the direction of the vacant shoe repair shop. "Ever since you bought this here building two years ago you kept raising the rent. Can't nobody afford it. Henry sure couldn't so you evicted him." The old lady's voice cracks with emotion.

Gerald looks in the direction of the vacant shop and vaguely remembers the old lady's husband. "He could have moved to another location. I have a business to run; this isn't my fault." The people standing outside shake their heads and murmur amongst themselves.

"Mister, he couldn't afford to move. This was *his* place for more than thirty years. Repairing shoes was his life and you took that away. It was too much for him so he...so he put a gun to his head. You killed him." The old woman cries.

The people milling about begin to talk to each other in angry tones and look at Gerald disapprovingly.

Gerald stands in stunned silence.

A young woman from the crowd walks up and gathers the old woman in her arms. "C'mon Mo'dear, don't let this stupid man upset you."

As the two women walk away, the old woman says to Gerald, "Don't worry, you gonna get what's coming to you. And it's coming soon. God will make sure of that."

Gerald gets into his car and quickly drives away. The old woman has rattled him. But, he can't let this encounter affect him for too long—it's just business and nothing else.

Chapter 5
BUSINESS AS USUAL

For the next few weeks Gerald's business takes up all his time, but he can't help thinking about his encounter with the old woman and what happened to her husband. On his drive to Lenox Towers in Buckhead, these thoughts float around inside his head. He frowns. At the red light across from Lenox Square mall, Gerald closes his eyes for a moment to clear his head for the meeting he has this morning. He takes a couple of deep breaths to focus. It's time to get down to business.

Gerald arrives at his office minutes later. It's a plush, tastefully decorated office with mahogany furniture and fine paintings of the Italian countryside. He barely nods a hello to his assistant, Karen. She says a tentative good morning as she eyes him running fingers through his graying temples, diagnosing his ogre mood in two seconds. She smiles nervously, quickly pours and hands Gerald a cup of Turkish coffee, the special brew he has directly shipped from Turkey. By the third sip, Gerald unthaws slightly. As if on cue, she hands him a list of business requests needing immediate attention and waits for his orders.

Gerald waves her away. "Karen, I'll let you know what I need in a few minutes."

She nods and goes back to her desk. He looks over the sheet while taking some more sips of coffee. Gerald looks back at Karen and smiles. "Thanks Karen, I needed this," he says, gesturing to his coffee cup. He takes another sip of the strong coffee.

"Any messages?" Karen shakes her head. "Is he here yet?"

She nods and says, "Yep. You know he is."

Gerald smiles at her and goes into his conference room where he shakes hands with a man whose big gold rings on his pinky and ring finger feel like brass knuckles. He is dressed in a tailored suit, a blue and white pin-striped shirt with the initials "T.V." monogrammed on the cuffs, and gold cufflinks.

"Good morning, Tony," Gerald says. "How's the new restaurant doing?" Tony sits down, placing his briefcase on the table.

"Great! Glad we could meet this morning. The deal can go through. Finally—it has taken long enough." Tony leans back in the chair, hands behind his neck.

Gerald sits down. "I wonder what made the Torres family change their minds now. I tried for a whole year to get them to sell."

"They had that bad inspection, remember? But, who cares, as long as they're selling now. We tear down that little restaurant, add it to the property next door, and start building our restaurants right away."

Gerald sits up in his chair and crosses his arms over his chest. "That seems strange. They've been in business for more than twenty-five years without ever failing inspection. Why now?" Gerald's mind went back to the day after the inspection. He had gone to the family to ask if Tony had harassed or threatened them.

Tony opens his briefcase and takes out some papers. "Why all these questions? This is how my family has been getting good restaurant locations for years. I know this like I know the back of my hand." Tony slaps the back of his meaty hands for effect as Gerald looks at him skeptically.

"I'm curious since the family had no problems until now, and were adamant about not selling. Something doesn't seem right." Gerald remembers the father and son had firmly said no, but there was a tightness in the air and a look in the granddaughter's eyes that said otherwise.

"This is business," Tony says. "They're the ones that need help—that little family place wasn't making money anymore. They can retire or go back to Cuba for all I care. This is how capitalism works."

Gerald blinks and smirks. "Tony, I know how business works. I'm not a kid in a sandbox. But, something doesn't feel right."

Tony says loudly, "I picked you as a partner on this deal, even though you have no restaurant experience. I also respect your business expertise enough to partner with your commercial property development company. You're good at what you do and I'm good at what I do."

"Yes." Gerald nods. "But, maybe we're taking this too far."

"You're in too deep; it's too late to back out now." Tony gives Gerald the papers before continuing. "And, I don't see how you can suddenly act like Jesus *now* after scoring big on our other deal."

There was a long silence as Gerald thinks about this. "That was different. That deal with the city didn't badly affect other people."

"That's where you're wrong, Gerald. That ten million dollar contract we got was because of you greasing the palms of the city officials. You stole money, took money from other businesses that followed the rules. Don't think you're not as greedy as me or any other businessman." Tony laughs sarcastically.

Gerald clenches his jaw. "You made your point." Gerald remembers two years ago when he bribed the city councilman.

The wind was blowing lightly as Gerald left the clubhouse and walked to his golf cart. His caddy followed closely behind with his golf clubs saying, "Today is perfect for golfing."

Gerald nods and looks up into the clear sky. "Yes, it's not hot at all."

Gerald was at the Sugar Loaf Country Club and playing for the Teens With AIDS Network Charity. His caddy puts his bag inside the golf cart while Gerald pulls out a new pair of black and white golf gloves from his pocket and tucks a small piece of paper inside the thumb of the glove.

Gerald looks around for a few seconds before a tall man with a thick moustache walks up to him with his caddy. "Gerald, I see on the sheet that your team is teeing off first."

Gerald instantly recognized the councilman and shakes his hand. "Hi, Dan. When is your team up?"

"We're the last to go. But that's okay, we plan on winning first place," Dan says, grinning as he pats Gerald on the back.

Gerald chuckles. "We'll see about that, my team always wins this tournament." They both stepped to the side away from their caddies.

Dan lowered his voice. "Hmm…your type always has to win." His smile immediately evaporates. "You have my money?" Dan asked.

Gerald handed Dan the new gloves. "I don't need any gloves," Dan says sharply.

"But, you need these. The bank transfer information is located inside. You'll get your two million dollars in three days."

The councilman smirks as he takes the gloves. Gerald says, "Oh, by the way, in case you forget to give me the contract, I have photos of you with your cute little college girlfriend." Dan's mouth opens in surprise. "I think you're paying her tuition at the University of Georgia. It would be a shame if your wife found out." Gerald walked away and climbed into his golf cart. Dan watched in shock as Gerald and his caddy drove away.

Tony breaks into his Gerald's thoughts. "Don't look so serious. I'm just not one to sugar coat anything. The city won't catch on, I made certain of that. Back to what's happening now—thanks to the Torres we have all the space on 14th street, and we can put up Trio. What other restaurant group has American, Italian and French restaurants all within the same complex connected to a concert facility? We're going to make history! End of story, so stop with all the questions. You're going to get what's coming to you, soon. All our hard work is paying off."

Gerald looks at Tony strangely, remembering that these were almost the exact words the old woman had said to him, "You gonna get what's coming to you. And it's coming soon."

Gerald feels uneasy as he flips through the papers. "You're right, it has never been done in Atlanta before."

"Ernesto, the father, will sign the contract later today. I'll have him come here before I meet with you," Tony says pointing to the papers. Then, flipping toward the bottom of the stack, he adds, "These are the final documents of my deal with your company. I'll have the check for you tonight at 7:30. Sorry to meet late, but I have a meeting at 5:30 p.m."

Tony gets up to leave. "Everything is all good now." He smiles. "See you this evening." Gerald walks him to the coor and shakes Tony's hand.

"See you later."

Tony leaves and Gerald paces the conference room for ten minutes. The words of the old woman echo in his head. He doesn't have a good feeling about this deal. Not at all.

Chapter 6
VALERIE AND GERALD

Valerie

On the other side of town, Valerie
Brooks has to prepare for a 7:30 meeting
and has been busy working all day. She
is running a little late because earlier her
mother came by unexpectedly, and the
two had not seen each other for several
weeks. Valerie walks through the door
with shopping bags and bumps into a
stack of books, spewing several lifetimes'
worth of advice across the hardwood
floor. *The Secret*, several Dr. Phil books,
and various other self-help books land on
the other side of the office desk. She
grunts, drops her bags, mad that her
quasi-Dewey Decimal system had been
disrupted. "Damn!" Valerie stacks the
books back in place then sits at her desk,
rubs on some hand sanitizer that sits
next to the computer. She takes a deep
breath and closes her eyes. Valerie is not
sure if it has been ten minutes or one
hour when she finally opens her eyes,
but she feels a bit calmer. She begins to
light candles in the office, living room,
and bedroom. Valerie's apartment is
spotless, decorated in monotone colors.
She didn't like clutter or bright colors so
her couch, table, chairs, and bed were all

cream colored that exactly matched her walls and curtains.

Valerie goes back to the computer, reapplies hand sanitizer and checks her schedule. She grabs one of her bags to make sure she has what she needs. While her emails load she fumbles through the shopping bag that contains Windex, hand sanitizer, anti-bacterial soap, and a box of condoms. She reaches into her other bag from one of the shops at the mall and pulls out a tiny red lace bra and panty set and some massage oil. She clicks on an email message on the computer screen: "One and half to two hours tonight is fine @7:30. I will bring an extra donation and champagne. Can't wait to see you again." She puts the lingerie on the desk, frowning. Valerie responds to a few more emails, then heads to the kitchen to put on rubber gloves and scrub down the apartment.

Valerie answers her door at 7:30 to Philip or Kent or Jerry, or whatever his name is. For one agonizingly long minute her empty brain searches for the correct name. She is tired and wants the client to hurry up and go home as soon as he's done.

Gerald

Gerald comes into Tony's office just as he's shaking hands with Ernesto Torres, head of the family restaurant they are buying. Ernesto looks at Gerald calmly which is a bit unsettling, but before Gerald can even say hello, Ernesto hurries out, leaving behind that same tightness from the day after the bad inspection.

Tony says, "What's his name...whatever..." Tony snaps his fingers trying to jog his memory then continues excitedly, "you know who I mean—the old man who just signed." He flashes a wide smile.

"His name is Ernesto," Gerald says, irritated.

Valerie

Valerie gets in gear to pretend *not to* pretend for an hour or so. Whoever he is stands in the doorway with a crooked, mischievous smile, drawling, "Hellooo babeee, don't you look like a big bottle of syrup!" His eyes greedily suck in every detail of her big breasts and slim waist, draped seductively in the red lingerie.

Gerald

Tony waves off Gerald's answer. "You don't sound excited. Your check for our other deal should change all that—it's instant gratification."

Gerald says, "I'm fine, just a little tired."

Valerie

Valerie gives a tiny smile. "Hi baby, how are you?"

"Hmmm, you don't sound excited," the clients says.

"I'm fine, sweetie, my throat is just a little dry." Valerie clears her throat, smiling bigger and forcing a twinkle in her eyes.

Gerald

Tony opens his briefcase and pulls out a check. "Per the the agreement for 35 percent ownership in your business…" He hands the check to Gerald. Gerald blinks at the four million dollar check for a few minutes. His stomach turns.

Valerie

Valerie's client hands her an envelope full of money. She says, "Make yourself comfortable," as she turns around and discreetly counts the $250 dollars before putting in her nightstand. Valerie turns back to him. "Are you ready to relax?" Then her stomach turns.

Gerald

After leaving the office, Gerald goes to dinner alone, barely knowing what he's eating, deep into his thoughts. Just as he walks through the door at home the phone rings. It's Tony calling from his car.

"Hey, Gerald, I just finished dinner with clients and wondered if you wanted to celebrate a little bit." Rock music is thumping in the background.

"I'm a little tired," Gerald says.

"I know. But this type of celebrating will actually perk you up." Tony chuckles. "There's a girl I see every once in a while that takes real good care of me." He pauses. "She looks good, long blondish-brown hair, great body and all, and isn't too expensive. But you wouldn't need to worry about that anyway." Tony laughs. "My treat."

This sounds like just what he needs. Gerald had frequently seen escorts when he had gone to Las Vegas and Amsterdam. "Okay, I need some fun." Gerald quickly grabs his car keys and heads to the door.

"Okay, I'll call her to make sure she's available. I'm sure she is. Just come to my office and we'll ride over there in my car."

Gerald leaves and drives to Tony's office.

Valerie

Valerie's client leaves and the phone rings as she's putting away the massage oil, lingerie, and other "work" items. She can go to sleep early for a change. A look at the caller ID makes her smirk.

"Hey, Sienna." That obnoxious, all too familiar voice saying her fake name irked the hell out of her.

"Hi, Tony."

"I want to swing by and see you real quick on my way home."

"I'm already booked," Valerie says. She hates seeing Tony. "I told you that I need at least an hour's notice. You always do this last minute thing with me," Valerie says as she counts all the money from today's work. It's not quite what she thought it would be and bites her bottom lip, counting again.

"Call your client to make sure he's still coming," Tony says. Then in a boastful tone, "I'm celebrating a big business deal I just closed with my business partner. He's coming with me so he can join in the celebration." She could almost see Tony strutting across the floor, sticking out his big chest, bobbing his head and preening like peacock. "And, you know you miss me."

Valerie grimaced as she thought about all the times he had come to see her—twice a month, almost every month for the last year. She thought he finally had stopped coming when she hadn't seen him for two months. She looks back at her stack of money not sure how she lost part of it, and realizes that she doesn't have enough to pay rent and may have to see Tony after all. But she wants to see if she can find another client to see her.

"Let me make sure he's coming and I'll call you right back," Valerie says.

"Okay."

Valerie hangs up and calls Jeff, one of her regular clients. She's relieved when he says that he can come over right away.

Valerie calls Tony. "Sorry, sweetie, he's still coming. Next time make an appointment so I can see you."

"Damn it, I'll set something up with you later then," Tony says disappointedly and hangs up.

Valerie quickly takes her "work" items back out, then showers so she can be ready when Jeff gets there.

Gerald

As Gerald nears Tony's office he thinks that maybe he shouldn't be seeing an escort with him tonight. He normally doesn't mix business with pleasure and a strong feeling tells him that this isn't the time to make an exception.

Gerald calls Tony. "Tony, you know what, I'm so tired I can barely keep my eyes open. I have to cancel on the fun."

"I was just about to call you. She was booked and couldn't see us anyway."

"What a bummer. Let me head back home and get some sleep." Gerald hangs up and drives home.

Valerie

Valerie is tossing and turning in bed with Jeff. He's extra frisky tonight, unsnapping her bra and tossing it on the floor next to the bed. Jeff's pudgy hands grope her breasts a little too roughly.

"Ouch!" she says. "Easy there, tiger."

"Sorry," he murmurs.

His big belly squishes Valerie as he gets on top of her. She gasps for air but doesn't have to wait long to breathe normally again because he finishes in a few minutes, then collapses on the side of the bed. Valerie turns away from Jeff. She doesn't look at any of her clients when they're done. *The things I put up with for money. Hurry up and leave already.* Jeff finally leaves. She sighs deeply and goes into the bathroom. Valerie turns on the shower and as she washes away his touch and smell she remembers the day she became a prostitute. It was thanks to Lisa, her high-school friend.

Valerie was in the bathroom at Lisa's friend's house. It was there that she "entertained" men. The light inside the small bathroom is dim as Lisa applies make-up to Valerie's face.

Lisa is one of the few friends Valerie has. They started hanging out together when Valerie played hooky from school one day and saw Lisa leaving, too.

Lisa squints as she brushes pink blush on Valerie's cheeks. "Almost done. Hurry, put this on. Our dates will be here any minute," she says and hands Valerie a tube of pink lip gloss.

Valerie puts on the lip gloss. Lisa smiles. "Great. Turn around and look," she says.

Valerie stares in the mirror at the thick foundation, blush, and mascara on her face. "I wish the lighting was better," she says. But, even in the dim light Valerie thinks she looks horrible. She frowns. "It's too much."

Lisa shakes her head. "You're just not used to wearing make-up. It's supposed to look like that."

"If you say so," Valerie sighs. She grabs a hair brush on top of the sink and brushes her long brownish-blond hair.

Lisa takes another brush and teases her long blond tresses. She poses seductively in the mirror, then unbuttons two buttons on her tight white shirt displaying the top of her extremely big breasts. Lisa is tall and looks like she's old enough to be out of college, even though both girls had just graduated from high school a few months ago.

Lisa wrinkles her nose at Valerie's yellow sundress with distaste. "That dress makes you even more like a baby." She adjusts the straps on Valerie's dress. "Good thing you don't have braces anymore, and that your date likes this sort of look."

"I've never dated an older guy," Valerie says nervously.

"It's no sweat. I've been dating guys in college since the ninth grade," Lisa boasts. Lisa was "fast" in high school— she "dated" guys several time a week, late at night and then would sneak back home when her father was drunk, passed out on the couch.

"I hope I do okay," Valerie says.

Lisa laughs. "You'll get the hang of it after the first few…dates."

"Well, I'm only going to do this until I get enough money to pay for college."

Lisa rolls her eyes. "I hated school, studying isn't my thing. Going on dates is way easier." Lisa puts a compact into her purse and puts the rest of the make-up underneath the bathroom sink. "You ready?" Valerie nods and they both walk into the living room.

Thick red curtains hang on the windows and there are several seating areas with red love seats and small white tables covered with glasses and bottles of wine.

The doorbell rings and two men enter and greet Lisa and Valerie enthusiastically. Valerie is surprised when she sees them. One man has sideburns and a full beard, like Lisa's father. The other man is bald and looks like her high school literature teacher.

"This is Hal," Lisa says to Valerie, pointing to the man with the beard. "And this is Frank." Lisa points to the bald man.

Valerie says hello to both of them, then whispers in Lisa's ear, "You didn't tell me they were old men. I thought they would be college guys."

"I told you they were older. These are my good regulars."

Hal eyes Valerie appreciatively. "You're the new girl," he says stepping closer to her. "How about a kiss?" Valerie is stiff as Hal takes her in his arms and kisses her. He smells like alcohol and cigars. "Loosen up, we're going to have a nice time," Hal says, holding her hand. Valerie sees the wedding band on his finger.

Frank loosens his tie and sits down. "Lisa, pour me a drink. I don't have all night."

Valerie whispers to Lisa, "Hal is married."

"So what?" Lisa angrily hisses in her ear then walks over to Frank, opens a bottle of wine, and pours some in his glass.

Hal plops down on a loveseat and pulls Valerie onto his lap. "I like you. I may have to take you shopping if you're extra nice." He starts to caress her back and leans over to kiss her. Valerie closes her eyes and pretends that she's somewhere else.

That happened more than fifteen years ago, but Valerie's memory of it is still vivid. She turns off the shower and begins to towel dry herself. She wonders how long she can stay in the business. Valerie hates what she does and hates herself. She has no idea if she can stop seeing clients, but knows she can't quit if she doesn't have a job. She wants no more Jeffs in her life, that much she *does* know.

Gerald

Gerald is tossing and turning in bed as he drifts off to sleep. He dreams of the old woman, Ernesto, his son, and the granddaughter.

The old woman is standing on the side of a dark street with a laundry basket in her arms. "Don't worry, you gonna get what's coming to you. And it's coming soon. God will make sure of that." She repeats this over and over again in a thin, gravely voice that eerily echoes down the street.

Then suddenly the Torres family is running down the street and Tony is chasing them in a black car, laughing while blasting rock music on his car radio. The street suddenly turns into a desert and then a cliff, and the family runs off the cliff. Gerald hears the screams and sees their flailing arms and legs as they hit the ground with loud thuds. Suddenly he is hovering over the lifeless body of Ernesto. Even in death he looks calm, with dirt, dust, and blood over his face like a veil.

The old woman appears, hovering over the dead bodies. She looks at Gerald and sadly shakes her head. "Look what you did. You gonna get what's coming to you. And it's coming soon."

Gerald wakes up, heart pumping and face covered in sweat. He hasn't had a nightmare since he was a kid. He tries to go back to sleep but finds he can't. Gerald wonders why he's so shaken up by a dream. He gets out of bed, opens his briefcase, takes out the check and throws it on the floor. There can be no peace with that money, with this business deal. A little voice inside him tells Gerald not to ignore the dream. Right then and there he decides to get out of business with Tony.

Chapter 7
GERALD'S OPEN DOOR & JOB SEARCH

Gerald

Gerald calls Tony and tells him that they need to meet. Tony comes to his office and Gerald breaks the bad news to him.

"What do you mean you don't want to be a partner anymore?!" Tony yells. He's so loud every vein in his neck and forehead is popping out like burrowing worms. He smashes his hand on the conference table in Gerald's office. Gerald jumps. He had already warned Karen, that there would be a scene this morning.

"Just what I said," Gerald says calmly, sliding the check over to Tony.

"You have no explanation? Is the money not enough for you?"

"It's not about the money. I don't want to do business with you anymore. I have a bad feeling about the Torres deal."

"Oh, it's something about that family. They don't matter. What's the big deal? Is this really worth jeopardizing our business deals?"

Gerald starts to speak, then stops. He looks Tony straight in the face. "I get the feeling that you forced them into taking the deal."

Tony laughs. "Did Ernesto tell you that?"

"No, he didn't. It's just a feeling I get."

"Feeling? A damn feeling! Go ahead and screw me. Why the concern over these damn Cuban people anyway? Here you go again trying to act like Jesus or something. Let me remind you that you love making money just as much as I do. We both made money off of the city contract. If the city was to find out about your bribes, we would get sued, face fines, and *you* would lose your good standing as a reputable businessman." Tony pauses to see if his words are affecting Gerald. Gerald stands there like a statue. Tony fires back up. "I promise that you will go down. I will make sure that your business goes nowhere. I will take you to court and nail you to the wall. I'll sue you for breach of contract for *two deals*!" Tony spits the words out.

Gerald looks at Tony. The flaring nostrils, the clenched fists. He looks like a rodeo bull. And Gerald was the cowboy that had fallen off and would never get back on. Gerald nods. "Okay." He walks out of the conference room. "Do what you have to do."

Tony storms out of the conference room and the energy left over is thick with rage, tension, and his loud cologne.

Gerald sits at his desk thinking about the drama that was about to unfold. Karen rushes in with a cup of Turkish coffee and a question on her lips. He waves her away. He's sure he did the right thing. But now he would have to face the repercussions of having chosen greed and the wrong business partner. There were signs before they did the city deal that Tony possibly had a dark side, but Gerald had chosen to think that Tony's other side was just light gray. Months earlier, Gerald shouldn't have ignored his gut feeling—the one he's listening to now. Gerald takes a deep breath and gets up from his desk.

He passes Karen as he leaves the office. She asks, "Is everything okay? I heard Tony yelling." Gerald barely nods. "See you later," she says. "I'll have all the reports done by tomorrow morning."

"Fine," Gerald replies. He sees Karen busy working on an Excel sheet on her Mac computer. She takes a sip of green tea from a cup, then reaches for a stack of papers on her desk waiting to be assembled in binders for the reports. Karen's eyes are puffy and her face is pale. Gerald eyes a framed photo of her husband and their smiling snaggle-toothed seven-year-old son, sitting next to the computer. Gerald stops and walks over to her desk.

"You know what?" Gerald pauses. Karen looks up, quickly opens up a Word document to take notes on what he needs. Gerald continues, "Take the rest of the day off and don't come in until noon tomorrow."

Karen's eyes widen in surprise and she sputters in her cup. She coughs and hits her chest a few times. "Did I hear that right?" Karen pulls open a drawer, fishes out a napkin, and dabs her mouth.

"Yes, you did," Gerald answers. "Are you okay?"

Karen looks at him in disbelief. "I'm fine. The accountant is coming by and I'm not quite done—"

"It doesn't matter, you need some time off. I know that you've been working late the last three nights." Gerald looks at the family picture on her desk. "See you tomorrow at noon." Gerald walks out the door.

Karen watches him walking away. "Thank you," she says.

But he has already gone down the hallway and doesn't hear her. Karen guesses that Gerald's giving her some time off had to do with what just happened in the conference room with Tony.

Valerie

Valerie is busy trying to find work. She's dressed the part for her interview, wearing a black business suit and carrying an attaché case she found in the back of her closet. She confidently walks out of the office of the Macy's houseware's manager, and into the small lobby, past people waiting to be interviewed.

The manager shakes Valerie's hand, then checks the text messages on her cell phone. "Thanks for coming," she says as Valerie smiles. "But, we're looking for someone who has experience in housewares."

Valerie's smile fades. "I have several years experience in women's clothing and I'm a quick learner," Valerie replies persuasively.

"The women's department doesn't have an open position currently. Check back in three months," the manager says and quickly walks away.

"Thanks," Valerie responds with disappointment as she watches the manager disappear down the hallway.

Valerie leaves. In her car, she looks at a long list of potential jobs she found on the Internet. She checks off the last item on the list, having already filled out online job applications or set up interviews for the entire list. Earlier that morning she tweaked her old resume, then went to the mall and filled out several applications. She had done retail sales several years ago while a student at Georgia State, so she was sure she could easily get a job at the mall.

Valerie's cell phone rings when she's almost home. It's a client. "Sure, I'm available," she says, then pauses. "Yes, I'll make sure to wear something sexy," Valerie replies provocatively, then hangs up. She frowns and shakes her head, then drives faster so she can get home and continue her job search before the client arrives.

Gerald

After Gerald leaves the office he drives to midtown and decides to stop by some properties he owns in the area. He thinks it's time for a change. To do something different and get his life back on track. His thinks about his mother—she's been gone for six years. When she was alive he wasn't that concerned about making money. But she's not here now and he has to figure out life on his own. He passes the Carter Center and heads towards Ponce de Leon Avenue. Driving past a big house he sees men and women walking toward the front yard. They're all wearing tattered and dirty clothes.

Gerald wonders why they're all going to that house. Looking in his rear-view mirror he faintly sees a sign but can't read it. Curious, he turns around at the next light to go back. He parks at the house and sees the sign: Open Door Community. He walks in and watches as men line up. Lee is reading from a clipboard. "Ralph." A man from the line answers, "Here." She continues calling names and the men respond. "Manuel...Cedric..." She finishes and says, "Okay, that's everyone on the list for showers. You can go upstairs now. There's plenty of soap and someone will assist you with fresh clothes to change into."

The men go up the stairs single file. Lee notices Gerald and comes over to him. "Hi, how are you? As you can see, this is shower time for men on Wednesday. Are you here to donate or volunteer?"

Gerald looks a little surprised and then quickly answers, "Yes, I am. My name is Gerald." He extends his hand to shake hers.

Lee smiles. "Pleased to meet you. That sounds great. So which will you do?"

Gerald smiles back. "I'll be donating money and volunteering. Just let me know what you need me to do."

Lee smiles and nods. "I'm so grateful for your help. We need both. First, let me show you around our happy home and I'll tell what we do here day to day for our residents."

Lee escorts Gerald to the dining room, the small but tidy kitchen, and upstairs to the residential area. Upstairs, Lee stops to speak to several homeless men. They all respond warmly to her. She explains, "We're a small house with only fifty beds for temporary residence, but we're open to a hundred twenty every day for food in the dining room." Gerald walks around the residential area, which consists of five bedrooms that each have beds that line the walls, small tables, and bookcases filled with books.

Going back downstairs, Lee shows Gerald the home's Harriet Tubman Women's Clinic and a foot clinic. "I'm impressed," Gerald says. "You have this place so well organized. I would never have guessed just by driving by all that's in this house. I thought a homeless shelter and soup kitchen would be in a regular building."

"We pride ourselves in making this place just like a real home, not some cold, impersonal living space for our residents. Let me show you the outside courtyard and then you will have seen everything."

Gerald likes the way she calls them "residents" and describes the house as a "happy home." It's obvious she has a deep respect for these people. She reminded him a little bit of his mother. This awakens something in Gerald, and then and there he decides to put a lot of his money and efforts into supporting such a good cause. Years earlier, when his mother was alive, Gerald had been an active volunteer alongside her. He stopped after she died and threw himself into his work.

Gerald and Lee walk outside as she tells him that the courtyard is open during the day for the homeless to rest and wait to get on the food serving list. Lee spoke to several people as they near the center of the courtyard. Then Gerald spots the old man going through his green suitcase. He is sitting in the corner. The man sees the two of them looking at him and shuts the suitcase. Loose pieces of red and white fabrics are hanging out at the corners. Lee waves to him, but the man barely waves back. She doesn't walk any closer.

"Aren't you going to talk to him?" Gerald asks.

"No...he likes to have his space and doesn't like people bothering him."

Gerald looks at Lee, sensing there is more than meets the eye. He looks back at the man and is sure Lee isn't afraid of him.

"What's his name?"

"I don't know. No one knows."

"You don't know his name?" Lee shakes her head. "That's strange."

"He refuses to tell anyone. He doesn't stay in the residence, but sometimes comes to eat with us. He likes to be alone, and we like to respect the wishes of the residents. So please don't bother him."

Gerald looks back at the man with the green suitcase and studies his face carefully. The man has been studying him as well, which puzzles Lee, since she's never seen him take an interest in anyone, especially a visitor. Lee remembers the vision he showed her and wonders how soon she will see her daughter again. But Lee has always been apprehensive about asking the old man if knows for fear he'll say no.

Chapter 8
VALERIE'S OPEN DOOR

Valerie is in bed with a client. He's cuddling her in his arms, her face is cradled in the crook of his arm. His thick chest hair prickles her nose. She sits up and glances at the clock on the nightstand. "Oh, look at the time. I have to get ready in a minute. I have another appointment."

"Time always flies when you're having fun," he says as he caresses her back. *And even when you're not*, Valerie thinks. He stretches his lanky frame closer to her and tries to pull her back down.

Valerie gently pushes him away. "I know, sweetie, I wish you could stay longer."

She slides out of bed as the client reluctantly gets up and puts on his pants, shirt, and shoes. She always has to spend extra time with him. He's very touchy-feely and likes to pretend that she's his girlfriend, which she hates.

He takes his wallet out of his pocket, pulls out a crisp fifty-dollar bill and folds it in her hand. "Here's extra for taking special care of me." He kisses Valerie on the mouth.

"Thanks," Valerie says with a forced smile.

As he leaves, he digs into his pockets, then looks on the floor. Valerie asks, "What did you drop?"

"They're around here somewhere," he mumbles.

Valerie spots a couple of blue pills on the floor near his feet. She points downward and he picks them up.

He grins and there's a twinkle in his eyes. "I can't have any fun with you without these."

The moment he leaves out the door Valerie groans and rolls her eyes. That's another thing she hates about seeing him—the Viagra keeps him going too long.

Valerie goes to her computer, then dials her phone. "I'm calling about the job," she tells the man on the other end.

"Thanks for calling, but we just hired a receptionist this morning," the man says. She hangs up in frustration.

Valerie flips her long brownish hair to one side, blankly staring at the computer screen. Getting a regular job was not as easy as she had thought it would be. She goes onto Craigslist to browse the retail job section. Some stores at Lenox Mall are hiring and she applies online, then she spots an ad for Victoria's Secret. "Oh, I'd be right for this one," Valerie says out loud to herself.

Valerie calls and gets an interview for 2:00 p.m. But when she gets there she finds out that the store manager's niece just back to town, and since she once worked there will get hired for the position.

Valerie decides to drive to midtown to see if she can spot some hiring signs. As she turns onto Ponce de Leon Avenue she comes upon a colorful sign on the front of a house and memories flood through her mind. It was the Open Door Community house. She vividly remembers this place as a teenager. Though she didn't stay there she had been there many times. Valerie slows down, then circles the block twice before deciding to park and go inside. She finds the office and asks someone walking out who to talk to about becoming a volunteer. Lee walks in behind her with Gerald and says, "Two new volunteers in less than a month, that's a good sign from God." She turns around. "Hi, I'm Lee, I run Open Door. How are you?"

"Hi, I'm Valerie, I'm great. How are you doing?" The two women shake hands.

"I'm good, thanks." Lee points to Gerald. "This is Gerald. He's a new volunteer." Valerie shakes his hand, then eyes him curiously, figuring him as a preppy Buckhead type of businessman. She couldn't picture him volunteering at a place like this. Usually his type served on the boards of charity organizations that held $500 a plate black tie events.

"I guess we had the same idea about wanting to volunteer," Gerald says to Valerie as he sizes her up. Pretty, not stunning like the women he usually dates. A nice body though. Professionally dressed, but not a businesswoman. Her suit definitely isn't a power suit.

"Yes, we did. It's good to help other people," Valerie says. "It's good for the soul."

Gerald looks surprised, not expecting that response.

Then Lee asks, "What makes it good for the soul?"

Valerie had said the first thing that popped into her head and came out of her mouth naturally. She now pauses to find the meaning. She looks at them both and answers, "Well, because when you help someone, you're helping yourself the most. You bring out the best in yourself, which will erase some of the bad in the world and the bad in yourself."

Gerald nods as his eyes drift faraway. A thoughtful look crosses his face, then he stares directly into Valerie's eyes. "I had never thought about it like that...and...I definitely agree." His eyes probe hers as if more truths linger in its depths. She quickly lowers her eyes and turns away.

"That's a great outlook to have, Valerie," Lee says. "I'd love to have you as a part of our family here. Let me give you a tour of the house."

"That would be great," Valerie says, smiling.

"Gerald, do you have time to go through the cleaning supply checklist right there? I'll be back in fifteen minutes." Lee points to a small table next to her desk.

"I'll be right here," Gerald says as he takes a seat.

Lee and Valerie leave. Gerald looks at the list, then writes a check for $4,000. He had already given Lee a check when he first started volunteering. Gerald walks to his car to check his cell phone for business messages and to put in his planner the dates he will volunteer at Open Door. On the way back in he goes through the courtyard and looks around—no one is there. He realizes he wanted to catch a glimpse of that strange man. He doesn't know why he's interested in the man but he is. Gerald hears a noise coming from the side of the house. He walks toward it and sees the sunlight bouncing off some moving muscadine bushes. He follows the noise and is surprised to see the old man with the green suitcase walking along the side of the house. Gerald walks a few steps and his loafers snap a fallen twig. The man immediately turns his head.

He yells at Gerald, "Why are you following me?!" He folds the suitcase under one arm, as if in fear that someone will grab it. He squints in the bright sun to see Gerald. Then his face and arm relaxes, and he lets the suitcase down by his side.

"I didn't mean to startle you," Gerald says. "I just heard a noise back here." They both stare at each other for a few moments. The man is very still. He is like an animal in the woods, cautiously observing a human intruding on his territory. For some reason this makes Gerald uncomfortable and he begins to shift from foot to foot, but he feels he shouldn't leave just yet.

Finally, he says, "My name is Gerald. I'm a new volunteer."

The man barely nods and mumbles, "Um, hmm."

Gerald picks a grape from the bush and rolls it between his fingers. "I was driving by and this place caught my eye. I'm glad I stopped by."

The man mumbles, "Hmm."

"I see that you're not much of a talker. Lee said you like to keep to yourself."

"Well, that's not happening much right now," the man says sarcastically, raising his eyebrows.

Gerald chuckles. "Sorry for disturbing you. I'll let you get back to whatever you were doing. Nice to meet you." He turns to leave, picking a few more muscadines. Gerald used to love to do this with his mother when he was a little boy. As Gerald picks, the air thickens around his face and chest. The muscadine bushes begin to shake around him and grapes jump down from their vines and spill onto his feet and the ground. He can feel heat move into the center of his chest, pulsating like an extra heartbeat. Gerald eyes widen with surprise and the old man's eyes glisten in the sunlight.

It was time again. This time the old man is calm and expectant, unlike normally when he is caught off guard as the visions come. The man touches one of the bushes, his hand begins to shake, then his arm, then his neck. The shaking spreads to his face, radiating into his wrinkles. Gerald stares, surprisingly calm. It feels like something that was supposed to happen.

The wrinkles begin to move off the old man's face and shoot light in front of Gerald. Images suddenly form, as if the man is a human projector, on the bush. Gerald sees a blurry image of a couple slowly appear. Gerald blinks rapidly because it's out of focus, then as it gets clearer he can see himself sitting in a restaurant, smiling. He's dressed in a dark suit and blue tie and is holding hands with an olive-skinned woman with long dark hair. He realizes he knows her. She's Christy Lockhart, an ex-girlfriend he once dated for two years. The next image is a close-up of her smiling eyes and lips. And coming from a faraway place, Gerald can hear his voice saying, "I'm the happiest man on earth." Next, he's holding a sparkling diamond engagement ring with a large heart shaped diamond surrounded by three smaller diamonds on each side. This didn't make any sense to him since his relationship with Christy was nowhere near leading to marriage. He had thought about marriage a few times in his life, but had never come close to proposing to any woman. The ring got smaller and smaller until it dissolved into nothing and all that was left to look at was a bush with grapeless vines.

And, just like that the vision is over. Gerald stands still, collecting himself. He blinks a couple times staring at the old man. He can't believe what just happened. Even though marrying Christy seems so far fetched, the vision was so real that he knows it must be true. The old man grunts, turns on his heel and runs away, along the side of the house.

Gerald yells, "Hey, wait a minute, come back!" He runs after the old man.

The old man's feet smash the muscadine grapes on the ground as he quickly runs. He turns slightly to yell over his shoulder, "Leave me alone or I will tell Miss Lee you're harassing me!"

Gerald stops and shakes his head in exasperation. He reluctantly turns around to walk back inside the house. Gerald hopes he can catch up with the old man later. He needs to find out more about what just happened to him.

Chapter 9
SOMETHING NEW

Gerald spends a great deal of his spare time at the shelter and soup kitchen. He also organizes fundraisers, donates more money, does repairs on the house, buys new appliances and beds, and recruits volunteers. He often works directly with Valerie; she has a lot of time to spend at Open Door since she still hasn't found a job.

Gerald proves not to be the typical Buckhead preppy businessman that Valerie originally thought he was. He likes to make jokes and gets along easily with her. Gerald is impressed with Valerie's intelligence and her concern for other people.

One day when Valerie and Gerald are fixing sandwiches for the lunch time meal, Valerie turns to Gerald and asks, "What do you do when you're not making sandwiches?"

"I'm a commercial real estate developer," Gerald replies. "And you, Valerie?"

"I'm, uh, a customer sales rep for an online cosmetic company."

At that moment Ralph, one of the residents, enters the kitchen and joins them making sandwiches. Valerie sets up the ice machine and the deli meat slicer, her usual routine. She rolls steel food preparation carts near the windows with yellow curtains. Gerald often teases her about how much of a neat freak she is. In the small kitchen the three of them form an assembly line: mayo on Wonderbread is Gerald, passed to Valerie for turkey and cheese, and Ralph finishes up with an apple and chips on each paper plate.

Passing the plate to Ralph, Valerie asks him, "When was the last time you saw your family?"

He hesitates a moment and says in a flat tone, "They don't want anything to do with me, haven't for years."

Valerie frowns, looking at him and Gerald. Ralph couldn't be more than thirty, but his face is hard and rough, like it had been dragged on a sidewalk.

"Maybe they've changed their minds by now," Gerald suggests. "Maybe you should phone and try to see them again."

Ralph looks at their caring faces with a crooked half smile. "Thanks for your concern, but I've been in and out of rehab for too many years. My folks and my sister and brother have pretty much written me off. He pauses. "I don't exist anymore."

Valerie asks, "You're off drugs now, right?"

Ralph nods. "For almost a year and a half. You know I can't stay here unless I'm clean. This is the longest I've been off drugs."

"That's good," Valerie says encouragingly. "But, still try to talk to your family. Family is everything," she says. "Even when we screw up, they're all we have. It takes some time apart for their importance to really become clear." Valerie reaches out to touch his shoulder.

Ralph touches her hand and says, "You're so sweet to care. But there's no hope where my parents are concerned."

After lunch Gerald and Valerie clean up the kitchen, then go outside and look at the radishes they had planted in the small garden. Valerie bends to touch the moist soil, then picks up an empty water can.

"Family is very important to you," Gerald says. "Are you close to them?"

Valerie looks up at Gerald then turns quickly away. "My father died when I was five. And my mother...I see her as often as possible." She fingers the dirt, the feel and the smell drifting into her mind unburying memories from long ago.

Valerie's fingers are in dirt and she's on her side. She moves and feels leaves crunching beneath her cheek. She gets up, brushes dirt and twigs from her ponytail and eyelashes, then slides back toward the water. Dirt is all over her, including inside the penny loafer still on her foot. She was running too fast near the creek and fell pretty hard. Valerie spits out leaves and dirt from her braces. She peers into the creek looking for the other shoe but can't find it.

Then, beyond the trees, on the street where she lives, an angry but familiar voice yells,
"Valerie…Val…Valerieeee…Where are you?!" She hears feet trampling through leaves and rocks.

"I'm over here, mom!" The footsteps are faster and closer now. Then she sees her mother, cheeks flushed from running, hair bouncing all over her head, scowl firmly sketched across her face, and hand on one hip.

"It's been almost two days, two days!" She holds up two fingers for emphasis. "You can't be gone that long." She looks Valerie up and down with disgust. "What the hell is wrong with you?! You look a mess. I don't want to even know what you've been up to. C'mon, let's go home." She grabs Valerie by the arm.

"Hey, did you hear me?" Gerald's voice breaks into her thoughts.

"I'm sorry, what did you say?" Valerie asks, blinking away the bad memory.

"I was saying that you slipped away for several minutes. I hope I wasn't getting too personal," Gerald says apologetically.

Valerie shakes her head. "I'm okay, I just don't want to talk about it right now." She rubs the dirt off her hands and turns to go back into the kitchen. Gerald follows inside.

He studies her for a moment. She has on no makeup and wears a pair of jeans and a t-shirt. She looks like "the girl next door."

"That's fine. I just didn't like you looking sad."

Valerie looks at Gerald and searches his face. She is quiet for a moment before saying, "That's a nice thing to say."

"Well, you're a nice person."

For some reason this makes Valerie giggle a little bit.

Gerald smiles. "I was wondering if you wanted to go out on Friday. He thinks, *I can't believe I just asked her out. She's not my type.* Gerald is curious about dating her though since she's obviously outside of his league.

Valerie opens her mouth to say no, then looks at him thoughtfully. "I don't think I'm really your type."

Gerald laughs, realizing she said aloud what he was thinking. "Look, I want us to go out and get to know each other better. Then, we can figure out if we're the right type for one other." Gerald discreetly eyeballs her big breasts and wonders how quickly he can get Valerie into bed and if she's any good sexually.

Valerie laughs, thinking, w*hat do I have to lose? He is a nice guy.* "That sounds great," she says.

Friday comes around quickly and Valerie has second thoughts about going out with Gerald. She paces up and down her bedroom as if she's in a hospital waiting room. Valerie looks through dresses in her closet, unsure what to wear. One dress is too low cut for a first date, unless you're Pamela Anderson. Another, too "third Baptist church" and only fit to wear when going to church with elderly relatives. Dressing for her occupation is much easier than dressing for a date. Being a prostitute she wears lingerie, but when dating, she actually has to wear clothes.

Valerie hadn't been on a real date in years. It's hard to have a boyfriend and sleep with other men at the same time.

Maybe she just shouldn't go out with Gerald. But it was too late. Gerald planned on taking her to a popular restaurant. What if she runs into a client? Is she really ready to start dating? Valerie stops questioning herself and finally picks a simple blue silk blouse and black skirt.

Gerald takes Valerie to Canoe, an elegant restaurant overlooking the Chattahoochee River. It was obvious he frequented the place when the maitre d' greeted him by name and asked if he wanted his regular waiter. This made Valerie even more nervous.

Gerald senses her nervousness as he looks at Valerie appreciatively. "You look pretty."

"Thank you, so do you," she says with a laugh.

"Do you drink wine?" he asks as he starts to study the wine list.

"Yes, I do." Valerie grins. "I've never seen anyone look at a wine list like they're studying for a final exam."

"They have a particularly great wine list here and I collect wine," Gerald explains. "So excuse me if I'm salivating." They both laugh. "What type of wine do you like?"

"I'm easy—I drink both white and red."

"Well, then I'll have to start teaching you all about wine."

Gerald orders a bottle of 1998 Chateauneuf du Pape Beaucastel to go with the rack of lamb and fennel he suggested they both try.

The waiter brings the wine, shows the label to Gerald, then gracefully pours a little bit in Gerald's glass for him to sample. Gerald sniffs then swirls the dark wine in the glass before tasting. After he nods his approval, the waiter pours the wine into a decanter. Valerie looks curious.

"Wine needs to breathe a while before drinking," Gerald explains.

"Oh," Valerie says. "My first lesson."

Gerald raises his glass. "A toast." Valerie smiles and raises her glass. "To great company and getting to know each other." They touch their glasses and sip the wine.

The waiter brings the rack of lamb dinner to the table with side dishes of steamed asparagus and fingerling potatoes. As they start to eat Valerie asks, "Where are you from? Your accent isn't Southern."

"I was born in Chicago. Moved here when I was three. Where did you grow up?"

"Near Six Flags. I went to that amusement park so often I know all the rides by heart."

"My mom used to take me there sometimes," Gerald says. "I loved riding the Scream Machine."

"Oh, me too! I'll never forget that ride. Does your mom still live in Atlanta?"

"My mother passed away six years ago," Gerald says, his voice sad with remembered loss. "She owned a small pottery studio and taught art classes for Emory's Continuing Ed Program."

"I'm sorry. I can tell you miss her."

"Yes, she was the best," Gerald pauses. "Valerie, I'm sorry that I brought up some painful memories about your mom back at the shelter. Do you see each other often?"

Valerie looks down at her plate, chasing a small piece of lamb with her fork. "I saw her recently. Mom can be a bit difficult."

"I'm sure you miss your dad."

Valerie nods. "I barely remember him since he died when I was so young."

He reaches across the table to hold her hand. "Mine left my mother right after I was born." Gerald takes a sip of his wine. "So, let's move on to more enjoyable subjects."

"Yes, let's…" Valerie says enthusiastically.

Gerald begins regaling her about his trips to Napa Valley and Bordeaux, France to visit the wineries. Her nervousness is soon forgotten when she discovers their mutual interest in food and books.

"I can tell you're a big time foodie," Valerie teases. "You have to be in order to pair great food with great wine."

"Yes, I'm a foodie." Gerald scratches his head. "Foodie. *Foodie*. Who invented that word? It doesn't sound masculine at all. It sounds like something women do when they're shopping at the mall."

"Gerald, I think the Food Network invented the word," Valerie says with a laugh.

"You're right. But, there needs to be another word for a male foodie. By the way, have you been to any of the food and wine events around town?"

"I went to the Taste of Atlanta a year ago, but that's about it," Valerie says. "I do love to cook though. And I have a terrific cookbook collection."

The waiter comes to the table with the dessert they had ordered, a strawberry-rhubarb cobbler with toasted almond ice cream and two spoons to share the delicious dessert.

"What other books do you like besides cookbooks?" Gerald asks.

In between bites Valerie answers, "Self-help and mystery books."

"My favorites, too. We'll have to compare our book titles soon." Valerie nods. Gerald is silent for a few moments as he stares at her and then says, "I think we may be each other's type."

Valerie stares back at him and smiles. "I think you may be right." They smile at each other and finish dessert.

Afterwards, as they wait for their cars in the valet parking area outside the restaurant, Gerald kisses her gently on the lips.

"Will you go out with me again?" Gerald asks.

"Of course, I will. You're my favorite male foodie."

Chapter 10
BACK TO THE FUTURE?

Gerald

Gerald keeps himself busy at work, knowing that any day his problem with Tony will rear its ugly head. It's just a question of when Tony will strike and how bad it will be.

Gerald walks into his office for an afternoon meeting. Karen hands him a stack of mail. "Gerald, your one o'clock appointment is running late.

"Thanks," Gerald says and takes the mail.

Suddenly, a man in a dark suit rushes behind Gerald. "Hi, can I help you?" Karen asks as the man puts a large envelope on top of the mail in Gerald's hand.

"You've been served," the man says and then hurries out the door.

Gerald is startled before he can respond. He opens the envelope and reads the letter from a law firm representing Tony. It states that that Gerald is being sued for 15 million dollars. He curses loudly.

"What is it?" Karen asks, looking at Gerald's angry, flushed face.

"That bastard Tony is suing me! Get Dennis on the phone," Gerald replies as he hastily walks toward his office. Karen puts his lawyer, Dennis through.

"Tony finally served me with papers," Gerald says to him.

"Can you come right over to my office?" Dennis asks. Gerald says yes and goes to his office.

Gerald walks in the door and sits across from his lawyer. "What is he suing for?" Dennis asks.

"Breach of contract for two deals and he wants 15 million dollars."

"Okay, we have to show a legal reason for you breaching the contract. I'll call my private investigator to dig up some dirt on Tony," Dennis says, picking up his phone.

Gerald shakes his head. "No, don't. We can't do that. I've done some shady deals with Tony that will definitely come out in court."

Dennis sighs. "Gerald, we have to have something to fight him with. What did you do anyway?"

Gerald hesitates. Dennis says, "Everything you say to me is protected by attorney client privilege."

Gerald takes a deep breath and looks embarrassed. "I bribed a member of the city council for two million dollars so that a government building contract got awarded to me and Tony."

"I see…"

"If I take him down, then I go down, too. There's no way to fight him."

"It'll be hard to win without any dirt on Tony," Dennis says. "Gerald, let me know if you change your mind. Meanwhile, I'll start preparing for court trial."

The next few days Gerald focuses on cautiously finding new business opportunities but he can't stop thinking about the upcoming confrontation in court with Tony. And he spends more time with Valerie at Open Door. It's a time to reflect and get his life in order. Ironically, this is what many of the people who live and eat at the shelter are trying to do, too. They're really no different than he is, he realizes.

Gerald often thought about that day when the old man showed him the vision in the courtyard of the shelter. Although Gerald has been staying away from the old man, he now decides to confront him once again in the courtyard. The old man is forced to stop. He's clutching the green suitcase and looks irritated, like a bee shaken out of a hive.

Gerald says, "I promise I'm not going to harass you. Please, I just want to ask you a few questions. You can't expect me *not* to have any questions after what you, uh, showed me."

The old man looks into Gerald's pleading eyes for a few seconds then says roughly, "Go ahead, but hurry up before I change my mind!"

Gerald begins his rapid-fire questions. "When will I see Christy again? I'm *actually* marrying Christy? When will this happen? Does she love me? I don't love her, so at which point will I fall in love?"

The man waves his hand at Gerald as if swatting a fly. "Too many damn questions. I don't control this." He points his crooked finger at his right eye and says, "What you see is what you see. I'm not an interpreter. I'm just the way you get the information you need to see."

Gerald is now even more curious. It's not every day you run into a homeless old man who gives you a powerful vision. As the man starts to walk off, Gerald asks one last question, "Do you give everyone visions?"

The man impatiently answers, "No. No! Now leave me alone. Don't talk to me again." He clutches his suitcase tighter and hurries away.

Gerald now believes there's a reason he was drawn to the Open Door shelter, and it was not just for the old man to show him visions.

Christy

Gerald is at a restaurant, meeting friends for dinner to help distract him from his legal fears and worries. As he walks through the bar area, he unexpectedly spots Christy sitting on a barstool sipping a glass of Chardonnay.

He goes up to her. "Hello, Christy."

She gives him a slow, familiar smile. "Well, well, well, I haven't seen you in awhile. How have you been?"

"Doing great. How about you?" Gerald smiles back. Low, blue lights at the bar allow him to see that she still looks good, regal as a Sphinx. Gerald notices her cream colored wrap dress that shows off her long legs. A few men nearby are eyeing her appreciatively.

"I just moved back to town," Christy says. "Got sick and tired of L.A. Didn't like the fake people and horrible traffic."

"And the smog," Gerald chimes in.

Christy raises her glass as if toasting. "And the smog. Give me Atlanta humidity any day." She pauses. "If your friends won't miss you too much, come join me for a drink."

Gerald looks around the crowded dining room and sees his friends already seated at a table near a window watching him. "Sounds good, I'll stay just for a minute," Gerald says as he sits down beside her and orders a glass of Cabernet Sauvignon."

"So, I'm back and will get into commercial insurance again, probably set up my own agency."

"Well, welcome back!" Gerald says dramatically.

Christy grins. "And you? How is business? Good as usual?"

"Business is doing what it needs to do," Gerald answers cryptically.

She questions him with her high arched eyebrows. "Interesting answer." She takes a few sips of wine.

"Truthful answer." He takes a few sips of wine.

Christy swivels her seat toward Gerald as her eyes rove over his body. "You've been working out? You look good."

"Yes I have, thanks." Gerald checks out her shapely body. "And you lock sexy, as usual."

"Thanks. I try my best," she says and winks at him. "Do you still own those apartment buildings in this area?"

"Yes, and they're doing great. Lucky I bought them before the housing market tanked."

"I agree. But you were always good at getting the right deal at the right time." Christy leans over and puts her hand on his thigh. "You did all sorts of *right* things with me," she says seductively.

Gerald fondly remembers the many nights they spent in bed together. "We had always had a good time, didn't we?"

"Oh yes we did."

A tall, suntanned man walks up to them. He looks at Christy with annoyance. "Who is this?"

Christy laughs and takes her hand off of Gerald's thigh. "Darling, so glad you got here early. This is my ex-boyfriend, Gerald. We were just catching up on...business." Gerald raises his eyebrows and smiles slightly. Christy turns to him. "Gerald, this is my boyfriend Brad."

Gerald extends his hand for a handshake. "Nice to meet you."

Brad nods, then looks at Christy. "Let's go, our table is ready," he says abruptly.

Christy finishes her wine, then gets up. "It was great running into you, Gerald." As Brad walks away Christy quickly whispers in Gerald's ear, "My number is still the same. Is yours?" Gerald nods. "Call me," she says and walks away.

Gerald watches as Christy follows Brad to their table. He will definitely call her soon. As he pays for their wine

Gerald wonders if Christy is meant to be with him like the old man's vision showed.

Gerald joins his friends at the table. One of the men says, "Geez, Gerald, since you made us wait you could have at least brought her over here and introduced us to her."

One of the women in the group looks over at Christy who's now sitting at a nearby table. "No, I don't think I want that much competition."

The others laugh, but Gerald still has a serious, slightly confused look on his face.

Chapter 11
MEETING AGAIN

Gerald phones Christy and asks her out on a date. She's so happy to hear from him. "Just thought you ought to know," she says, "I'm not really involved with Brad. He wants to get married and I'm not interested. Besides, he's not ambitious enough for me."

Christy is beautiful, and they have, or had, great physical chemistry. But, Gerald now realizes that he never really liked her. "Like" perhaps wasn't the right word. "Connect fully" was probably a better description. But then, Gerald has never really connected fully with any woman. He treats women well, but something is always missing. Gerald and Christy didn't even have a bad breakup; they just sort of drifted apart because of their busy schedules. But a great deal had just recently changed. The vivid reality of the vision—wait a minute, was it reality?—has confused Gerald. He doesn't want to push into a future, he wants it to unfold. Christy was always setting up business meetings, putting her ideas into action, and trying to pull him into that mix. It's how she's always been. Gerald now senses that he needs something different from a woman and even though he wants to sleep with Christy, a little voice inside his head tells him to cancel their date.

Christy doesn't take Gerald's rejection seriously and keeps calling with any excuse to see him. Whenever she mentions she will be near his office coming from an appointment or near his house at the end of the day, Gerald can almost feel her breath through the phone with the weight of her expectation. But he decides to wait. To wait for...to wait for something to happen that would truly be a sign for him to pursue Christy again.

* * *

During the next several weeks when Gerald works at the Open Door he actively looks for the man with the green suitcase. But he's nowhere to be found.

"I thought Lee said that he never talks to anyone. Why are you so interested in him?" Valerie asks one day when they are both cleaning up in the kitchen.

"I just want to talk to him, like I do with the other people who come here. You have to be curious about a man that nobody knows his name."

"I think you should just leave him alone. You may find out some things that even he doesn't want to remember."

Gerald realizes that Valerie's observation is quite perceptive. "Okay, okay. I won't pester him. I promise." He pecks Valerie on the cheek as he heads out the door.

"I'll pick you up at your place, say around seven-ish?" Gerald says.

"Good," Valerie says. "I'll be starving by then." She laughs as Gerald heads to his car.

Gerald pulls into the Cactus Car Wash up the street, tells the attendant he wants a premium wax and detail, then goes into the waiting room.

"Oh, that looks sweet!" Gerald exclaims as he spots a photo of a red 911 Porsche Boxster on the cover of a *Car and Driver* magazine. He briefly looks out the window and sees a flash of green, then looks back at the Porsche photo. Gerald does a double-take and looks out the window again—this time he recognizes the man with the green suitcase. The man is talking to one of the attendants and Gerald wonders what he's doing here. The attendant looks stern, shakes his head and pulls a toothpick from his teeth. The old man looks disappointed, turns and begins to walk away. Gerald goes outside and walks up to him.

"Hey there, what's going on?"

The old man stops, turns slowly and answers reluctantly in a harsh tone, "What are you doing here?"

"Uhh…the same as everyone else," Gerald says.

The man looks around, shrugs and walks off. Gerald has to quicken his pace to keep up.

"Stop following me," the old man says without turning around.

"Is everything okay?" Gerald's concern is genuine.

No answer.

"Is everyth—"

"Stop talking to me." The man still doesn't turn around.

Gerald walks in front of him, blocking him. "I just want to help."

Then a loud voice yells behind them, "Hey, don't be messing with the customers. I told you we don't need to hire anyone." Startled, Gerald and the old man turn to see the attendant who had just been talking to the old man. The attendant is scowling and still picking his teeth with the toothpick.

The old man quickly starts walking away, mumbling something. Gerald quickly says to the attendant, "He isn't bothering me, I know him." The old man looks at Gerald in surprise.

The attendant looks at the man, then turns back to Gerald. "Oh, okay. I thought he was annoying you. We don't like street folks to come in here."

Gerald frowns and responds in a tight voice, "I'm fine. By the way, I just realized I won't be needing a wax or detail after all. Just give me a wash."

The attendant is irritated. He nods. "Fine, whatever you want, sir." Then he walks off.

Gerald looks at the old man. "I don't like rude people, especially ones that chew on toothpicks."

The old man stares at Gerald a few moments, then grumbles, "Thanks. Anyway, *you* are the one that's bothering me."

Gerald chuckles. "You're right." He pauses. "I have a little proposition for you. Since they wouldn't hire you, I'd like to pay you to wax my car."

The old man tips his head to one side skeptically. "I don't need your help. Why are you being nice to me?"

"One, my car needs a wax. And two, I try to be nice to everyone. Remember, I do volunteer at a place you go to a lot."

The man's face relaxes a bit. "How much are you paying?"

"Is twenty okay?"

The old man's eyes light up. "Yes, that's fine. But, where can I do it?"

"Good question. There's no room in the back of Open Door. Let's see..." Gerald looks up the street. "Hmm..." Then he snaps his fingers. "The Kroger grocery store parking lot is a good place. We'll park in the back and nobody will bother us there." The man nods in agreement.

After twenty minutes Gerald's gold Mercedes E550 sedan is brought around and he pays the attendant. The old man puts his green suitcase on top of the seat and begins to sit on it.

"Oh, don't sit on it; that's not comfortable," Gerald says. "Put it in the back."

Gerald reaches for the suitcase and the man jumps and quickly snatches it off the seat, clutching it tightly to his chest with both hands. "Don't touch that!"

"I'm sorry. I was just moving it so you could get in."

The man eyeballs him fiercely for a moment. Then he relaxes, moves the green suitcase down from his chest, and puts it on the floor of the passenger seat before getting in the car. They drive off as the car wash employees exchange puzzled looks. The old man shifts around, looking down at both sides of the seat, rubbing his dingy blue pants and fingering a big hole in the knee.

"I don't think I should be in here without me sitting on my case or you putting something down to keep your car from getting dirty," he says to Gerald.

"It's not a problem," Gerald assures him. "You're just fine."

The old man shrugs. "Suit yourself."

At the rear of the Kroger grocery store, Gerald gets out of the car and removes a clay bar, wax, and shammy cloth from the trunk. He hands them to the man. "I'm glad you can work on my car. But I have one condition, you—"

"I knew it! I knew there was a catch. Let me be on my way." The man shoves the items back into Gerald's hands and starts to walk away.

"Wait, wait—you don't understand. The only condition is that you tell me just a little about yourself."

The man's eyes penetratingly search Gerald's face, as if some other truth was deeply embedded there.

"Hmmph." He grabs the clay and shammy and begins to rub the clay on the car in a circular motion with the towel. "I will tell you just a little bit. Because that's all there is to know."

"At least just tell me where you're from. That's not too private, is it?" Gerald asks gently.

"I mean that just a little bit is all I know. I don't know where I'm from," the man says.

"Because your parents moved around? Or you were adopted?" Gerald asks. "That doesn't matter. Well, where were you raised?"

"I don't know."

"What do you mean you don't know? What city did you live in growing up? Where did you go to high school?"

The old man stops rubbing the car. "I mean that I don't remember."

"What happened? Were you in an accident that made you lose your memory?"

"I don't know."

Gerald begins to rub the back of his neck, looking at the old man in confusion. "That doesn't make any sense. You have to know if you were in an accident."

The man sighs and says slowly and angrily. "Like I said, I don't know. I don't know. I actually don't remember beyond two years ago."

Gerald stares at the man and can see in his face that he's telling the truth.

Several minutes pass, then a car honking its horn jerks Gerald back into the conversation, but all he can say is, "Okay."

"That's all there is to know, so there is never a need for you to bother me with questions ever again," the man says adamantly.

They stand together in silence. Gerald wishes the conversation hadn't turned out like this. When the old man is almost finished polishing the car Gerald asks him, "You can't find out through a vision who you are?"

"I can only show visions to other people," the man says softly.

Gerald nods and there is more silence. The man is now finished and hands the clay and shammy to Gerald. He takes it, then says, "I have a question about my vision. In it I was proposing to my ex-girlfriend. I'm confused because, though we dated for awhile, we weren't close to getting married. And now I'm dating someone new and I really like her. I don't know... what's going on. Is this real, will I be marrying my ex?"

The man looks at Gerald hard for a long moment. "I have nothing to do with what happens to you." He pauses. "I'm done, can I get my money?"

Gerald reaches into his pocket and hands a twenty-dollar bill to the old man. "Thank you," the old man says as he reaches into the car, grabs his green suitcase and walks out of the parking lot and down the street.

Gerald watches the old man disappear into the crowds of people on the sidewalk. He wonders about the old man's memory loss and his special gift. "They must be connected," Gerald mumbles to himself.

Chapter 12
CHAMPAGNE AND A MOVIE

Gerald has been going back and forth with his lawyer about the court case. Gerald can't take the stress anymore and calls Dennis. "I want to settle with Tony to avoid a trial."

"Are you sure about this?" Dennis asks.

"I'm sure. I just want to get this over with," Gerald says firmly.

"Okay. Let me call Tony's lawyer and see what can be worked out."

Later, Dennis calls back. "Bad news. Tony refuses to settle," he says tensely.

Gerald sighs. "Well, then court it is." Gerald is deeply disappointed as he hangs up.

Gerald decides to ask Valerie out if only to get away from his problems. He calls her and she says she can see him tonight. "Great. I want to take you to something that I'm sure you've never experienced, a sabering event."

"Hmm...is it like jousting?" Valerie asks curiously.

Gerald laughs. "It does involve a sword, but it has nothing to do with jousting. It's about opening a bottle of champagne."

"I can't wait to see it," she says, intrigued.

"I'll pick you up later."

He escorts Valerie into the opulent St. Regis Hotel, which despite its elegance still retains an air of casual comfort. Valerie says, "This place is gorgeous. I can't wait to see the demonstration," Valerie says excitedly.

Gerald smiles broadly. "I think you'll like it."

They head upstairs and go into the wine room. Valerie smiles upon seeing row after row of great wines housed in tall, clear cabinets, framed in white wood.

"I've never been to a champagne sabering before. Have you tried this at home?" she teases Gerald.

Gerald smiles. "I love to saber a bottle of champagne on New Year's Eve."

"So you have a big sword at your house just for opening champagne?"

Gerald laughs. "Well, a saber isn't a big sword. At least, not the one used just for champagne. It's only about two feet long. And yes, I do have one at home."

"I'm impressed," Valerie says.

As they move through the wine room an attractive man in a dark suit walks up to them. "Hi Gerald, I haven't seen you in awhile. Are you here for the 6 p.m.

sabering?" He has a thick European accent.

"Hi, Scott." Gerald introduces Valerie to the St. Regis's wine sommelier.

Scott looks at his watch. "Excuse me, I must run—I start in about five minutes."

Scott walks to the front of the wine room. A small crowd of people are waiting for him to begin. One of the hotel staff hands him a saber and a chilled bottle of Moet champagne. Scott tucks the saber under one arm and looks at his small audience. "Good evening, everyone. I will now demonstrate champagne sabering. Please don't try this at home—it's dangerous if you haven't been trained to do this properly." He tilts the Moet bottle in his hand and unpeels the foil on the neck of the bottle. Then, Scott slides the saber up and down from the middle of the bottle up to the neck. "Sabering was done in the 1800's by Napoleon's troops. When celebrating victories they would use their swords to cut open a bottle of champagne to drink."

With a quick and graceful flourish of his wrist, he cuts the bottle at the neck and some champagne drips on the floor. Gerald and Valerie clap along with the tiny gathering of people. The hotel staff pours champagne in flutes for everyone.

The crowd raises their glasses for a group toast before drinking. Scott thanks everyone for joining him and then walks over to Gerald and Valerie, who congratulate him on his excellent "performance."

Gerald says, "I've seen him do this to a hundred bottles in a row."

"Whoa," Valerie says.

Scott leaves, saying to Gerald and Valerie, "Have a wonderful rest of the evening."

"I was thinking about us having dinner here at the hotel's restaurant," Gerald says to Valerie. "Would you like that or do you want to go somewhere else?"

Valerie looks at him. "I really can pick another place?"

"Sure, I don't always have to pick where we eat dinner."

Valerie smiles. "I'm just used to you planning all our dates." She pauses. "Okay. You know, I would really like to go to the movies. There's a dinner movie theater not too far from here, near Lenox Square mall."

Gerald stares at her in surprise and says hesitantly, "O...kay." He finishes the rest of his champagne in one gulp.

"I'm sorry." Valerie looks nervously at the disinterested expression on his face then at his slacks and dress shirt. She quickly says, "I know we're a bit dressed up for the Fork and Screen—"

Gerald interrupts. "No, no. Let's go see a movie. That's a great idea. Matter of fact, I haven't been to a movie in over a year."

At the Fork and Screen Gerald has a surprisingly good time. After they go back and forth about what to watch Valerie promises not to pick a "chick flick." They finally decide on *Salt* starring Angelina Jolie. They eat burgers, fries, and chicken fingers and Valerie teases Gerald that this is probably what they would have eaten at the St. Regis."

"Minus the wine list," Gerald says.

Valerie passes ketchup to Gerald and he asks, "Where's the maitre d'?

"I'll go get him," Valerie replies. They burst out laughing and someone shushes them. They quiet down and enjoy watching the movie.

Gerald takes Valerie back to her apartment and walks her to the door. They are laughing as Valerie steps under the night light over her door to dig into her purse and find her keys.

Gerald steps closer to her and puts his hand over hers. He leans close to her face. Valerie turns her face up to his, her blue eyes gleaming. Gerald softly touches her cheek and lips with his fingers and leans in slowly to kiss her. She puts her hands around his neck and holds him close as they kiss intensely for several minutes.

Finally, Gerald lifts his head and looks at Valerie. They are both breathing heavy. Her hair is slightly tousled. She looks at him from underneath her eyelashes.

Gerald is aroused and just as he is about to ask her if he can come inside she pushes him gently away. "I know you want to come in," Valerie says as she nervously smoothes her hair back into place. "But, I'm not ready for that."

"Okay, there's no pressure," Gerald says even though his eyes are pleading.

"You're not upset, are you?" Valerie asks with a worried look.

"No," Gerald says with disappointment and then takes a deep breath to calm his racing pulse. "There's no reason to be, I had a good time tonight." He kisses her gently on the lips and traces the tip of her nose with his finger. "We both have to get up early for work. So, I'll say goodnight."

As he reluctantly steps away, he says provocatively, "But if you change your mind just call me." Valerie gives him a subdued smile in response.

Inside her apartment, Valerie pauses in front of the living room window. She listens for the sound of Gerald's car as it leaves the driveway. Valerie continues to stare out the window. She glances at her watch and sort of wishes that Tony wasn't coming to see her in an hour. She had wanted to invite Gerald in, but...but, it was weird, actually wanting to sleep with a man who wasn't her client. And it was weird really liking a man. It had been so long since Valerie had spent quality time with a man that she had forgotten how good it felt. But she wasn't ready to take the next step.

Tony calls to say he's on the way to her apartment. Valerie goes through her work items, overlooking massage oil and candles since he didn't like either one of those things. She pulls out the condoms. Tony likes to get straight to it. Valerie sighs.

Later, in bed, Tony is doing it too hard, as usual. And, unfortunately, she forgot to buy lubricant. The headboard and the nightstand were shaking almost in unison. Her vagina was sore already and he was nowhere close to being done. She hates his cologne, it smothered her nostrils as he lay on top of her. She hates him. Hates herself. Valerie felt the cheapest being with Tony, like a dirty old nickel on a laundromat floor. But he saw her often, though he didn't tip and always wanted a discount. He is on top and she looks over his shoulder and thinks of sienna. Not her fake name, the color. She chose that name because it was soft, gentle. It was earth and leaves, and most of all, peace. Peace. She was Sienna but she wasn't sienna at all. She moaned, staring hard at the ceiling, looking at the squiggly lines on the plastered ceiling. One. Two. Three...in her head she counted them until her pretending finally wore off and tears silently slid down her face. Finally, he finished and she ran off to the bathroom as if she needed to pee really bad, but it was really to wipe away the tears.

Afterwards, as she walks Tony to the door, he says, "I'll see you next week around the same time. I have extra stress to relieve since I'm dealing with getting screwed by my former business partner."

Valerie searches his face for a few minutes as if she has never laid eyes on him. And then she says slowly, "No, that won't work."

"Okay, then what day and time?"

Valerie swallows hard. "As of right now I'm out of the business." Her mind suddenly feels clearer. A light comes to her eyes.

Tony looks as if someone threw a glass of ice water on him as Valerie closes the door. She leans against the door, with a deep sigh, hoping she did the right thing since she hasn't even found another job yet.

Chapter 13
THE NIGHT ISN'T OVER

Gerald thinks about Valerie on the drive home. He wipes his mouth and sees the smudges of dark pink lip gloss on his fingertips. He really wanted to sleep with her. With other women, he would've already been sleeping with them by now. And, if it hadn't happened he would've been upset. But, with Valerie, for some reason he wasn't that upset. He couldn't put his finger on it, but there was something different about her.

Gerald yawns as he enters the gate of his subdivision. A beautiful golf course sits across from his house. The security guard at the booth greets him. Gerald nods in response as sleepiness suddenly weighs heavily upon him. It had been a long day.

Gerald goes inside his house which looks like a page out of an interior design magazine. Artwork from Italy and France adorn the walls and priceless antique chairs and tables are in each room. He heads to the office to look over some papers before going to bed. He begins reading but then nods off for a few minutes. Laughter fades in gradually from a faraway place in an oncoming dream. Gerald wakes up with a start. He groggily stumbles around the big mahogany desk piled with tabbed folders, bumps into the matching bookshelves filled with business books, and bangs his knee into the bronze sculpture of Abraham Lincoln in the corner near the door. "Ouch." Gerald gingerly rubs his knee, the pain matching the loud metallic sound the sculpture made when he bumped into it. He heads to his bedroom.

The Old Man

Near the #6 bus stop, the old man tiredly plops down on his normal spot under the street light. He had walked for three blocks to get here. He settles on the grass, opens his suitcase and pulls out some crumpled, dirty newspapers. The old man puts them on the grass and lays his head on top of the makeshift pillow as he stretches his body out next to the green suitcase. "Ouch." He grabs his knee in pain. This wasn't the usual arthritis twinge. This feels like something metal hit his knee. The old man looks down at his knee, then feels the grass around him. He sits up, looks to the left and to the right, and across the street and sees nothing. He lies back down. The sounds of the occasional car driving down nearby streets and the crickets night-time serenade close to his ears help him to drift off to sleep.

Deep in sleep the old man feels his body moving up and away from his grass bed. His body stands up. He's stands on something…something firm, but soft. He bends to put his suitcase down and touches what he's standing on. It's a carpet. He hears breathing of someone across from him. He can smell…smell—it isn't the usual smell of his sweat and dirty clothes. It was the smell of clean. He isn't near the bus stop anymore. He's in someone's bedroom.

The old man's eyes aren't open as he sleeps on the grass, but, he can see inside the bedroom. It's dark, with a sliver of moonlight peeking through a crack in the curtains at the window. It's enough to light the room. The old man sees the outline of someone sleeping in a big four-poster bed under white sheets. He steps closer. It's Gerald.

The old man's mouth turns down in a frown as he shifts on the grass. "*Damn it! I can't get away from that man, even when I'm asleep.*" Suddenly, heat and energy pour out of his chest like water out of a spout. His body shakes. Even though the old man's eyes are closed he sees the brightness through his eyelids, and covers his eyes. His wrinkles begin to move and itch and he scratches them. He feels the brightness of the energy hovering over his face like a low, thick cloud.

The old man tries to wake but finds he can't. He feels the energy slowly but purposefully move toward Gerald. Once the energy reaches him, Gerald begins to dream. The old man's frown deepens as he realizes this isn't his normal asleep— he's giving Gerald a vision at the same time too. "Damn!" the old man curses aloud as his head twitches on the crumpled newspapers.

Gerald

As soon as Gerald's head hits the pillow sleep comes to him. One side of his mind senses someone is in the bedroom staring at him from across the room. One the other side of his mind, dreams float closer to him like ocean waves on a shoreline. Whoever is in his room steps closer to the bed. Gerald can tell that the person is irritated. Gerald isn't scared. He knows instinctively the person won't hurt him.

"Damn!" a male voice curses. Gerald instantly recognizes the old man's gravely voice.

Suddenly, Gerald feels a burst of energy coming from the side of his bed— from the old man. The energy pushes down on Gerald, heavy like a weight. He sinks into the bed until he falls out of the bottom and lands feet first inside a very bright room. He squints and covers his eyes because it's so bright. There's a large window completely filled with the sun. It's as if the room is sitting directly inside a ray of sunshine. The old man is outside the window, his face is glowing, the wrinkles moving, alive with beams of sunlight. His chest also emanates with sunlight. The green suitcase is next to him and the pieces of red and white fabric sticking out of it glow like fireflies at dusk on a summer night.

Gerald asks, "What's going on?" The old man doesn't answer. He asks again. There's still no answer. The old man's unblinking eyes stare back at him.

Gerald looks at his hands and the rest of his body. He's infused with the sunshine coming from the old man. The entire room is a piece of sunshine. Gerald isn't sure what this place is. He looks around the room. There's a brown sofa with an Oriental rug in front of it. A woman encircled in darkness is on the floor digging through the old man's green suitcase, oblivious to Gerald standing there. The sunshine doesn't reach the woman and Gerald can't see her face, so he leans in to see her better. She throws shirts, underwear, and other items in a big pile onto the floor. The woman gets up and turns toward him. The sunshine begins to penetrate the darkness surrounding her, like a spotlight. It moves up her arm, her chest, and just as it gets to her face, the woman disappears.

Then the room becomes dark as if a switch has been turned off. But, Gerald is still bright with sunlight. He walks carefully across the room to see if the old man is outside the window or if the mystery woman has reappeared in a different part of the room. Once again, Gerald hears the same laughter from when he was awake in his office. It's not the old man's voice. It gradually gets louder until it sounds like it's playing on surround-sound speakers. Then, Tony appears directly in front of him sitting on the brown sofa, sunlight spotlighting him.

Tony laughs, flashing his white teeth in a sarcastic smile as he says, "Bankruptcy is bad, but you'll be okay. Bankruptcy is bad, but you'll be okay." His lips move over and over again repeating the phrase like a skipping CD.

Gerald covers his ears and screams, "Shut up!"

Tony keeps on, "Bankruptcy is bad, but you'll be okay."

"Nooo…damn you!" Gerald runs toward him, charging with balled up fists. His fist connects with Tony's face. He feels the bones in Tony's cheek beneath his knuckles. The bones crack like walnut shells. The sunlight from Gerald's fist slices through Tony's cheek and Tony evaporates into the air.

Gerald screams, "Come back! Come back, you bastard!" Breathing heavily like a wild beast, rage seeps from every pore of Gerald's body. He walks back and forth hoping Tony will come back so he can beat the crap out of him.

After a few minutes, he calms down and that's when the room brightens again. A light breeze blows across his face. Gerald looks back at the window. It has disappeared along with the old man. Gerald looks at his hands and body and sees that the sunlight has left his body. He looks to see if the old man will reappear. He doesn't. He's by himself.

The Old Man

The old man wakes up angry yet happy that the vision has stopped so he can get Gerald out of his mind. He finally goes back to sleep—this time there are no more visions and the old man drifts into a dreamless sleep.

Gerald

Now he's sees trees and bushes are all around. Gerald is outside in the garden behind Open Door. The tops of radishes peek up from the garden beds. Something rustles through nearby bushes a few feet away. Out of the bushes the old man runs in his direction. He runs straight through the garden and rudely tramples the radishes. A loud voice behind the old man yells, "Stop right now!" followed by two cops who run after him. They disappear around the corner as the garden shakes and bright sunlight bursts from the radish tops. Gerald closes his eyes and his body floats up in the air.

He's awake. Sitting up, with his elbows propped on the pillow, breathing rapidly. Gerald's eyes adjust to the dark bedroom. Gerald turns on the lamp on the nightstand. He runs his fingers through his hair remembering every detail of the dream. The old man— interesting that he dreamed about him. And who was the disappearing woman? Then Tony, his worst nightmare, had appeared. Tony's loud laugh and mocking words creep inside Gerald's head. *Tony is going to try to destroy me.* Gerald turns off the light and stares into space, unable to fall back to sleep.

Chapter 14
GOTTA GO

The big, lawn-sized trash bag sits in the middle of Valerie's living room and is filling quickly with all the tools of her trade. Everything was organized in categories before she tossed them, even though it shouldn't have mattered since they would be going into the same outside garbage can. Victoria's Secret g-strings and teddies, massage oils, and various sex toys are being thrown into the bag. Then she strips her bed, vacuums, and scrubs the bathroom thoroughly. Valerie then deletes ads on the "Backpages" online magazine, a Webcam site, client address book, business contacts, and calls the cell phone company to change her number to a new and private one. Finally, the last and hardest thing to do: she calls Marisa, her closest girlfriend in the business, to break off their friendship. There is no answer and Valerie thinks about calling later. Marisa would try to talk her out of quitting. She had major financial problems and clung to Valerie like a sister since she was the only "normal" person Marisa had contact with since getting into prostitution. Valerie couldn't think about her anymore though. She takes a deep breath and leaves the "dear John" voicemail. "Much better," she says to herself, she feels lighter and her mind is clearer. Everything will work out fine and she'll find a job soon. Her thoughts can finally flow freely like water from a spring.

Gerald spends less time volunteering at Open Door. With Valerie he's distracted and even disinterested.

"Gerald, are you okay? You seem so preoccupied lately," Valerie finally asks him one day when they're serving lunch at the Open Door.

"I'm fine..." He hesitates. "I'm in the middle of some important business, that's all."

Valerie shakes her head. "I'm not trying to be nosy, but there's something you're not telling me."

Gerald turns away from her probing eyes. "Everything is fine. *Really.*"

"Then why can't you look me in the face?"

He shrugs. "I just don't like being questioned about my business deals."

Valerie takes his hand in her hand. "Listen. I'm worried about you. I can tell that something is wrong. I care about you."

Gerald sees the concern in her eyes. "Thanks, sweetie. Please don't be concerned. I have a little snag in a business deal. It'll be okay." He squeezes her hand reassuringly then kisses her on the forehead. "By the way, I care about you, too."

Valerie smiles and sees in his eyes that Gerald doesn't really think everything will be okay. She hopes that maybe later he will tell her what's really going on.

Gerald knows there's no way he can tell Valerie that he may be losing his business and his money. "I can't stay long. I just came by to drop off some kitchen supplies and some money for Lee. I'll call you later tonight."

Valerie nods and watches Gerald as he heads to Lee's office. When he comes out of the office, Gerald walks right by the old man but doesn't notice him. The old man looks at his worried face and automatically knows it has to do with the dream vision.

He has been secretly observing Gerald the last couple of weeks whenever he sees him at the shelter. He wonders why in the hell he keeps giving Gerald visions. The old man normally just gives one vision to someone, never several visions to the same person. It's not like him to get rattled, but this is a problem. There's no way of knowing when or if another vision will be given to Gerald since the old man has no control over the visions. But, the old man has control over himself and decides to take action.

Over the next two days, the old man begs for money in the same Kroger grocery store parking lot where he waxed Gerald's car. Then he finds an old DVD player and a television set that someone threw into the dumpster behind the store and pawns them. He goes back behind the grocery store, makes sure no one is around and begins to carefully count his money. The old man dumps crumpled one dollar bills, quarters, dimes, nickels, and pennies on top of his suitcase. It takes him a few minutes to count. He mumbles, "97...98...99...and...45 cents." The money totals $99.45. He wraps all but $2.00 in an old shirt and puts it inside the suitcase, then stuffs the $2.00 in his pants pocket.

The old man walks to corner of N. Highland and Albion Avenue and boards the #3 bus. He gets off near Spring Street and walks a few blocks until he gets to the Greyhound bus station where a bus has just pulled in.

The sign on the front reads, "Chicago." Some black girls get off and wait for luggage to be loaded off the bus. They get their luggage and drag it straight from the curb to the Magic City strip club across the street. Beady-eyed junkies and African taxi drivers waiting for fares, watch this female parade that features bulging butts hanging out of booty shorts and breasts stuffed inside tube tops.

The old man walks to the entrance of the Greyhound station. The loud screeching of a car badly in need of new brakes causes him to turn around. He sees a scowling young woman with a long green scarf tied around her head get out of a beat-up Oldsmobile. The tailpipe is dragging and one window is duct taped. Loud rap music blasts from the radio.

She yells at the man driving, "Turn that damn music down!" He rolls his eyes and adjusts his baseball cap low on his head before turning the volume down. "While you're having a good time, if the rent is not paid in two days we will be on the street."

"I know, baby. I'm working on it I got it covered."

"Yeah right." She waves her hand in anger and frustration and hurries inside the bus station. The man immediately blasts the music again and drives off.

Inside the crowded station, the old man looks at bus schedules for several cities. He's not sure where he wants to go, but he knows he wants to get away from Gerald, far away. Gerald asks too many questions. Then, he remembers the Chicago bus outside.

Aloud he says, "Chicago it is."

Chicago wasn't a place to be homeless in the winter time. He overheard someone at the shelter say that everyone from Chicago calls the winter wind "the hawk" because it was so fierce it cut through you like a knife. The old man knows he can handle it—he's tough as old cured leather.

The old man stands in the ticket line. The woman behind the counter keeps looking at the clock behind her. Her agitation is building. It's the old man's turn in line just as the woman who had been in the beat-up Oldsmobile now steps behind the counter.

The other woman says, "Girl, you're late again! You know I gotta get outta here to pick up my kids."

"I'm so sorry. I'll work overtime for you one day to make it up."

The first woman shakes her head. "That's cool, Sheryl, but this is the third time you're late. I don't want to do it, but I'm talking to the supervisor. Maybe she can switch you with someone else."

She quickly walks away as Sheryl curses under her breath and mutters,

"Oh God, I hope I don't get fired." She puts her purse under the counter and looks at the old man. "How can I help you?"

"What's the price of a senior citizen ticket, one way to Chicago?"

Sheryl taps some keys on the computer. "Which part of Chicago?"

The old man answers, "Downtown."

Clickety-clack go her fingers on the computer keyboard. "It's $97.00."

The old man looks worried and asks, "Is that including tax?"

Sheryl looks up from the computer. "Yes."

The old man sighs with relief even though that only leaves him with 45 cents. "What route makes the least stops?"

Clickety-clack go the keys again. She sighs loudly and answers snippily, "The 7:30 p.m., 1192 route has no transfers.

"Is that route cheaper since it has no stops?"

Sheryl says, "No! Listen, while you're having a good time asking a million questions, other people need to buy tickets." She rolls her eyes and taps the counter with her long fake French manicured fingernails.

The old man opens his suitcase to get the shirt with the money. He counts out

$97 and hands it to Sheryl, putting the leftover change back in his pocket.

Sheryl barely raises her head as she prints the ticket. "Are you checking any luggage?" He shakes his head. "Line up behind door 13 an hour before the 7:30 p.m. departure time to catch the bus."

She hands the ticket to the old man. He frowns and snatches it from her and puts it in his suitcase. He snaps, "I saw you outside. Remember, you're only half a step from being on the street just like me." He walks away. Sheryl's eyes flicker with surprise and shame.

With only 45 cents in his pocket he wonders how he will eat. Maybe someone on the bus will buy him some food once he gets to Chicago. There's nothing the old man can do about it now.

He goes to the bathroom to pee. A man comes in and uses the urinal next to him. The man can barely pee straight because he is scratching one arm vigorously. The old man looks out of the corner of his eye and sees he's one of the beady-eyed junkies he saw outside Magic City. He quickly relieves himself and picks up his suitcase.

The junkie looks at the suitcase and points. "Hey man, you got stuff hanging from your suitcase. Put it back inside."

Before the old man can stop him the junkie grabs the suitcase and pulls the red and white fabrics that are hanging out. The old man quickly grabs the suitcase away from him. "No!"

The suitcase flies open and a burst of energy hits the junkie in the face. He screams in pain, "Ahh!"

At the same time two other men come into the bathroom as the old man scrambles on the dirty floor to close the suitcase. A loud voice asks, "What the hell—?"

The junkie holds the left side of his face. "My eye, my eye. Something from that suitcase hit my eye! I'm going to sue. I'm calling O.J.'s attorney what's-his-name."

The old man yells, "You shouldn'a touched my stuff!" Then he runs out of the bathroom and rushes outside the Greyhound station to the startled looks of waiting passengers. He clutches the handle of the suitcase so tightly his knuckles turn red. The old man goes across the street and stands near the strip club.

It's hot outside and he wipes his hand across his sweaty brow. He sighs and mumbles. "At least at Open Door I didn't have to deal with junkies."

After about thirty minutes he goes back inside the Greyhound station to stand in line at door 13. The line is long and winding. An announcement on the intercom blasts, "Attention in the terminal. Your 7:30 p.m. schedule for Chicago is now boarding behind door 13. Please have your tickets ready to hand to the driver when he comes to the door."

The old man opens his suitcase to get his ticket. He fumbles through shirts, handkerchiefs, and other knick-knacks and can't find it. At 7:20 p.m. the bus driver walks through the door, goes down the line to take tickets and people walk outside to board the bus. The old man frantically looks again in the suitcase and still can't find the ticket. At 7:25 p.m. he rushes back to the bathroom and searches for the ticket on the floor near the urinal. But, he knows it's not there. He was outside for too long. He's sure that one of the men in the bathroom stole the ticket.

The old man walks back to the line. The clock reads 7:30 p.m. The bus driver and all the passengers are gone. He goes to customer service center to see if anyone had turned in the ticket, but he knew no one had. He stares at a sign that says, "Greyhound is not responsible for missing and lost tickets."

Clutching his suitcase, he goes out of the bus station and sits on the curb. No money. No ticket. The old man scratches his head. "What am I going to do now?"

Chapter 15
LAWSUIT, COMING BACK, AND RADISHES

At the Greyhound station, the old man sits on the curb for several hours. He's surprised when Sheryl comes up to him and asks, "You missed your bus; are you okay?"

The old man does a double-take, then answers sharply, "Why do you care?"

"Look. I'm sorry," Sheryl says softly. "I really am. I'm not a bad person. I'm just having a bad day. You look like something is wrong."

He looks closely at her and sees the sincerity in her eyes. "Someone stole my ticket."

Sheryl purses her lips. "I'm sorry. I wish I could replace it, but I'd get fired for giving you another ticket for free. I'm in enough trouble at work."

The old man smirks. "I heard earlier."

"Let me see what I have." Sheryl pulls a shabby black wallet out of her big purse and empties the contents. Then she digs into the bottom of the purse and gives him $1.81. "That's all the money I have, I know it's not much."

The old man's eyes get big. "Ohh."

Then Sheryl hands him a plastic bag. He looks inside and sees a bag of pretzels and an apple. "It's left over from food I brought with me to work."

At that moment, screeching announces the arrival of her ride. The car pulls up to the curb and she quickly walks away from the old man. As she jumps into the car he says, "Thanks."

Sheryl doesn't hear him though because the man driving asks her in a nasty tone, "Why were you talking to that homeless man?"

"He's cool," Sheryl replies. "I was just telling him that he missed the bus." The car pulls away from the curb with a belch of smoke.

The old man is touched that Sheryl gave him what she had—he knows she's facing eviction. He asks someone nearby for a quarter so that he can catch the local Marta bus. The old man doesn't want to be here anymore. This unfamiliar place isn't lucky for him. For some reason he thinks it wasn't meant for him to leave town anyway. Time to get back to his territory. That night he sleeps at his usual spot near the bus stop.

He's on the street until the grime on his body causes him to itch. The old man asks someone what day of the week it is. It's Wednesday—shower day at the shelter. He slowly, reluctantly walks toward Open Door because he doesn't want to run into Gerald. The old man changes his mind and turns around. He stops to collect his thoughts. Aloud he mutters, "I'm not going to let one man stop me from doing what I want to do." He figures Gerald will be too preoccupied like he was the last time he saw him to cause any problems. He turns back around, quickens his pace and walks with purpose. The old man is lost in his thoughts and doesn't notice a patrol car driving by. The cops look at him curiously for a few moments, then look at each other. They slow down but don't stop as the old man walks inside the shelter's courtyard. They talk to each other pointing at the old man, then drive away. The old man walks into the courtyard and waits to get on the shower list.

Gerald leaves his office and drives to the shelter. His cell phone rings. A few minutes earlier his lawyer Dennis had called about the court case taking place in two days and Gerald assumed he was calling back with some additional information.

Gerald answers the phone as he pulls into Open Door's driveway. "Things are about to go from bad to worse for you, Gerald." His mouth opens wide as he steps out of the car. He drops the phone

on the gravel driveway but quickly picks
it up. It's Tony.

Gerald brushes off the dirt before he
puts the phone back up to his ear. Tony
asks, "You there?"

Gerald walks toward the courtyard.
"I'm here. I have nothing to say. Have
your attorney call my attorney."

"Shut up and listen!" Tony yells. "I
know about the shoe repairman that
killed himself and the properties you own
in the poor neighborhoods."

Gerald stops dead in his tracks.
"What!?"

Tony continues, "I think the Atlanta
Journal newspaper would love to hear
about this."

Gerald is quiet for a moment, then he
says, "You bastard."

"Not only will I beat you in court,
you'll lose business once this information
goes public." Tony pauses and says
sarcastically, "You'll go bankrupt.
Bankruptcy is bad, but you will be okay.
I told you I would destroy you." Tony
laughs loudly. Click. He hangs up.

Gerald turns off the phone and stares
at nothing while the courtyard fills with
homeless people. Some shuffle by and
speak to him but he doesn't hear them.
Gerald feels dazed, something has come

over him, like a fog after a heavy rain. He bows his head to think.

Tony's laugh. The same from the dream. Those words: "Bankruptcy is bad, but you will be okay." The same from the dream. The exact same.

Gerald looks up and sees the old man walking into the courtyard. He stares at him hard. Gerald remembers that the old man was in his dream. He blinks quickly, then it hits him in that instant, *the old man gave me the vision while I was dreaming, he was actually there with me.* Realization spreads quickly over his face.

The old man feels someone's stare searing into his back. He knows who it is before turning around. He meets Gerald's stare. The old man sees the gleam of recognition glowing in Gerald's eyes, like a kid that just found out that Santa Claus is really mom and dad. Gerald knows he gave him the dream vision. The old man's gaze doesn't waver and hardens like flint. He thinks, *Yeah, that's right, I gave you another vision. Don't ask no questions. Go away, damn you.*

Gerald winces as if the old man hit him. Blood rushes to his head. Gerald's heart beats in his ears. Both men are very still. Their eyes lock like cowboys in a gunfight showdown. The tense moment is broken when Lee comes outside. "Hi everyone, the list is starting for the shower and a change of clothes. The old man slowly turns away. Gerald goes inside. He heads to the kitchen to check the vegetable garden supplies—he's going to do some planting and weeding later.

The old man feels much better after he takes a shower, changes clothes, and eats a meal of baked chicken, mashed potatoes, and green beans. He runs into Eddie in the dining room.

Eddie grins broadly when he spots the old man. "How've you been? Haven't seen you in awhile."

"Good," the old man answers. "You got any jobs lately?"

Eddie nods. "I've been working on a construction job and it's looking like it may turn into something that will last for six months. One of the volunteers here let me use their cell phone so the company doesn't know I'm homeless."

The old man's eyes light up and he smiles. "That's great."

"I'm glad, too. I'm saving so I can pay for a small place, so I don't have to be on the streets. Maybe you can stay with me?"

The old man looks surprised. He didn't see Eddie often, and didn't know that much about him. "You know I like being alone."

"I know you do," Eddie says with a smile. "You don't steal from me, you don't talk a lot, and you keep to yourself. In my book that's a good friend and I like helping friends."

The old man tilts his head to one side and looks at Eddie, then lowers his head. "That's nice, but I can't live with you...or anybody."

"Well, the offer still stands," Eddie says cheerfully. "Once I get my place, you may change your mind."

The old man scratches the side of his nose and looks uncomfortable. "Well...I gotta go. See you around."

"See ya." Eddie waves.

The old man leaves the courtyard. As soon as he walks onto the sidewalk the two cops who had seen him earlier pull up. The one in the passenger seat jumps out in front of the old man. "Hey, it's him. I told you." He turns to look at his partner and they both nod in agreement.

The old man looks startled. "You got me confused with someone else. I didn't do nothing."

"I know you didn't," the cop says. "A few months ago you turned in some stolen items. I just want to ask you some questions."

The old man curses under his breath, then takes off running toward Open

Door. The cop runs after him while his partner parks on the side of the curb and joins in chasing the old man. The old man runs down the driveway and heads through the back of the shelter and into the garden.

Gerald has just stepped back into the kitchen with a bowlful of radishes and snap peas he just picked from the garden. Other volunteers and residents are outside. Gerald hears the sound of running footsteps and sticks his head out the door to see what's going on. The old man stoops behind some bushes to catch his breath, but starts running again when he hears the cops closing in on him. He runs right past Gerald through the garden trampling on the radishes. "Stop right now!" one of the cops yells out.

The old man keeps moving and zig-zags through the front of the house next door and disappears in the back. The cops lose him and stop the chase. Breathing heavily, and after they catch their breath, the cop says to his partner, "Why is he running? He did a good thing turning in that stolen stuff. Nobody else would've done that." They head back to their car. The conversation is overheard by two huge men who look like twins standing nearby. People from the courtyard and garden follow the cops and look to see where the old man went. Eddie is among them. The two huge men walk by him. Eddie remembers seeing them at the shelter. They have matching scowls on their faces. Eddie hears one say to the other that they were "going to get the old man" for turning in the stuff they stole. Eddie frowns and hopes his friend will be okay. Whatever is going on doesn't sound good at all.

Gerald goes back into the garden. Dirt is everywhere. Radishes are all over the grass beyond the plant beds. Everything was exactly like in the dream. The old man's visions were perfectly accurate. But, why were the cops after him? What had the old man done? Gerald hoped it wasn't anything too bad. But one thing he is certain of: the old man has a connection to him for some strange reason, and it's getting stronger each day.

Chapter 16
GOOD NEWS, BAD NEWS

On the way to Open Door Valerie drives past a nearby store and notices a help wanted sign for sales posted inside the window of Trendz Boutique. She decides to stop in and apply for the job. The store is filled with women's trendy casual clothes, handbags and costume jewelry.

Beth, the store manager introduces herself to Valerie and looks at her application. "Good. You have several years experience in women's retail," Beth says obviously impressed. She's a cute, petite blond woman with a short bob haircut and is wearing a purple ruffled blouse and blue jeans.

"Yes, I enjoy working retail very much."

"Our store gets very busy so you have to constantly be on your toes and be helpful to customers at all times. Do you have references?"

"Yes, I do. I volunteer up the street at Open Door three days a week—I was on my way there when I saw the sign in the store window."

Beth nods. "Trendz donates food and volunteers at the shelter's Christmas dinner every year." She pauses, smiles and says, "I'm going to hire you. Can you start tomorrow?"

Valerie beams. "Yes, I can. Thanks so much."

"Well, then," Beth says, "come in at 3 p.m., the store owner will be here."

"I'll see you tomorrow."

Valerie hops into her car feeling a wave of genuine joy and relief as she drives to Open Door.

Gerald is at his office getting his business affairs together. He realizes that once Tony calls the Atlanta newspaper about the shoe repairman, his business will lose a lot of money. What's more, Gerald doesn't have much hope of winning the court case tomorrow. "I'm afraid you'll probably be out of a job in a few weeks," he says to Karen. She responds with a sad nod. Gerald talks to his financial advisor to liquidate some assets and to his attorney about selling the commercial properties he owns in the poor neighborhoods. He leaves the office, calls Valerie and leaves a message when she doesn't answer.

Valerie leaves the shelter and quickly drives to Gerald's house. She had just gotten his voicemail in which he wanted to explain about his business dealings with his partner. He sounds relieved and anxious.

Valerie rings the doorbell and waits a few moments but when Gerald doesn't come to the door, she rings two more times and peeks through the window. She sees the huge flat screen TV turned on but Gerald isn't sitting on the brown leather couch in front of it. To the right, the light is off in the dining room. She knocks on the door impatiently. "Hellooo!" Finally, Gerald runs to the door and opens it quickly.

"Val, sorry about that." He kisses her. "I was in the office on the phone with my lawyer." Valerie gives him a worried look.

"Things could be better," Gerald says seriously. He sighs. "Come in, get comfortable. I just opened a bottle of wine; would you like some?"

"A glass of red would be great," Valerie says as she takes off her shoes. Gerald comes into the den with a bottle of Cabernet Sauvignon and two glasses.

"How was your day?" He sets down the bottle and pours Valerie a glass of wine.

She takes a sip of wine while he pours himself some. "It was great. I start a new job at Trendz Boutique tomorrow."

"Terrific," he says. "But I didn't know you were looking for a job."

"I got tired of working...from home."

Valerie takes another swallow of wine. "Your day sounds like it was hectic. What's going on?"

Gerald runs his hand through his hair. "Let's see—where should I start?" Gerald sips his wine pensively. "I got into a partnership with a man who had—shall we say—questionable business practices," Gerald says. "I didn't have proof. I just had a bad feeling. He runs a restaurant group and I partnered with him on a huge deal."

"I didn't know you were in the restaurant business," Valerie interjects.

Gerald sips his wine. "Well, I'm not. But I was briefly. We had just closed on a big business deal. This happened right before I met you." He looks away from Valerie. "Also, we had done a different deal two years ago that was not...totally legal."

Valerie nods. "Oh?"

Gerald looks at her and quickly says, "But it was nothing like what I suspected him of doing with this new deal. I'm not innocent in the other deal. I also own commercial properties in poor neighborhoods where I...uh...I charge high rent. And, a tenant...killed himself because of this. I take full responsibility for my actions."

Valerie shakes her head. "Gerald, I'm not here to judge you, that's not me."

"Well, anyway, I suspected that my ex-partner threatened a family that owned a restaurant and property that he bought. He said he didn't." Gerald frowns. "I didn't believe him. So, I backed out of that deal, plus another deal where he was buying into my main business. He's suing me for breach of contract. We go to court tomorrow. And, to make matters worse, he's going to the Atlanta Journal newspaper to tell them about the tenant who killed himself. I wanted you to know before the press came out. My business will be destroyed and I probably will lose everything. I've done some bad things. This was bound to catch up with me. I hated keeping this from you but I didn't want to upset you."

Valerie says, "I'm glad you're telling me now. You're not a bad person. It's awful what's happening to you. But you're not alone. I'm here for you no matter what. I'm going with you to court. What time do I have to be there?"

Gerald hugs her tightly. "You're the best, but I don't want you to go. I don't want you caught up in this mess. The press may be there waiting for me."

"I still want to be there."

"Wait a minute, your first day at the new job is tomorrow. I don't want you to get fired before you even start."

"Don't worry. The manager isn't there until the afternoon. Forget about my schedule. I'm there tomorrow to support you."

Gerald gently kisses Valerie and smiles. He pulls back and his elbow knocks over a glass of wine. They both jump. "Damn!" He quickly walks to the kitchen.

"I can get rid of the stain," Valerie says as he comes back with a sponge, carpet cleaner, and club soda.

Gerald hands the items to her and laughs. "Oh I forgot, you're better than any cleaning lady I've ever had."

Valerie dabs club soda on the stain, then carpet cleaner and scrubs hard. "Oh yeah...the carpet won't look too bad..." Her voice fades away as she scrubs, remembering something from long ago.

Valerie's mom says, "I don't what's wrong with you, why do you do these things?"

She opens the door to their house. They walk into the kitchen and step over pots and pans, plates, newspapers, cans of salmon, and boxes of Jiffy corn muffin mix strewn on the floor. The curtain in the kitchen window is hanging off the curtain rod and below it the sink is piled with dishes. The refrigerator door is open and mostly empty except for a gallon of spoiled milk.

"Mom, I'm sorry. I really am."

Her mother looks at the mess and shakes her head. Angrily she says, "I come home to this. You're as dirty as this house from being at that damn creek. Stop running away and making a mess. I don't have time to clean up after you!"

Valerie's mother steps into the dining room. There are school books stacked up on the table: American literature, biology, world history. Notebooks sit next to them. She opens up a notebook and reads a letter that is typed on her high school letterhead. She waves the paper in the air. "I see your grades are slipping. You have two F's and the rest are D's. Well, now I know. You have to buckle down and study more. You used to get good grades."

"I promise, mom, I will do better." Valerie tugs at her ponytail.

There's a spilled glass on the table. Underneath the table, on the floor is a dark stain. "Oh, for the love of Jesus, is that grape juice you spilled?" Her mother picks up the cup and smells it. "Yes, it is." She throws the cup back down on the table and sighs deeply.

Valerie quickly says, "I'll clean it up now. The carpet won't look too bad."

"You drive me crazy," her mother screams. Clean this carpet, this table, the kitchen. Clean this entire house. I want it spic and span!" She calms down and her angry tone subsides. "When you're done, then do your homework." She walks away in a huff.

Valerie goes to the kitchen and runs some water. She gets a sponge, some Comet cleaner, and fills a bowl with cold water. She goes into the dining room, gets on her hands and knees and scrubs vigorously at the grape juice stain on the carpet. She hates grape juice anyway.

Gerald breaks into her thoughts. "Valerie, when you clean it's like you're in a trance."

Valerie blinks a little to get back into the present moment.

She smiles. "All done. You can hardly tell it's there."

"Can I hire you to replace my regular cleaning lady?" They both laugh. "Naw, you work much better as my girlfriend. Now, how about some veal meatloaf? Are you hungry?"

"Yes, I am. That sounds delicious!" Valerie follows Gerald into the kitchen. "I'll make the salad," Valerie says opening the refrigerator and taking out a package of arugula, a container of grape tomatoes, a cucumber and a jar of Greek olives. As she starts making the salad, Valerie glances at Gerald from time to time and thinks about what he has ahead of him tomorrow at court. She hopes everything works out in his favor but fears the worst.

Chapter 17
THE HOMECOMING

A woman wearing oversized dark black sunglasses is standing next to a car in the parking lot of the Kroger grocery store. A tangerine and white scarf is wrapped around her head, tied gracefully at the neck. She's wearing white linen pants and a silk white top and looks as if she should be lounging poolside eating bon bons. The woman is on her cell phone asking to talk to "David." A voice asks, "Who is this?"

"Tell him Chantal is calling."

There's a long pause. "He's...not here. I'll tell him you called, Chantal."

Chantal frowns and hangs up. Chantal walks into the grocery store fanning herself with her hand. The sun is like a schoolyard bully, pestering and relentless. She's grateful for the relief of air conditioning. She tightens the silk scarf around her head as she frowns at some diet bars. She picks them up anyway, then goes to another aisle to get several bottles of Perrier. She hums a few bars from a popular French song as she stands in the check-out line. Chantal eyes a Vogue magazine, and picks it up, too. The check-out girl scans her items in between picking at some big pimples on her cheek.

Chantal wrinkles her nose in distaste as she notices the girl's zit riddled face and says in a haughty tone, "Picking at them only makes them worse."

The girl rolls her eyes and answers sarcastically, "Thank you sooo much." She looks at her cash register screen. "That will be $12.65."

Chantal sniffs and lets out a disapproving, "Hmpf!" She adjusts her large black sunglasses on her nose, then fumbles in her quilted white Chanel bag to get her wallet and gives the girl a twenty-dollar bill.

The girl gives her change and Chantal says snippily, "Use a good cleanser. A woman's face should always be beautiful and flawless." She flounces off and the girl eyeballs her angrily.

As Chantal walks out of the market she hears a man's voice say, "Please don't come back in here. I know it's hot, but you can't come in here."

She looks to her left and sees a man in a blue button down shirt with matching tie and black slacks with a name tag that says, "Ed Herman—Store Manager." He's talking to a dirty old man with a green suitcase. The manager points in the direction of the door. The old man quickly walks out and goes up the street.

Chantal walks to her car parked in the back far from other cars. She gets in and opens a bottle of water. She tightens her scarf before drinking then leans her head back on the headrest. Chantal takes off her glasses and lays them on top of a Vogue Paris magazine open halfway on the passenger seat. The leather is cracked like a scorched desert and she runs her fingers inside the lines of the splits in the leather. Chantal hates the ugly American car—it's so beneath her. Hopefully, she will get another luxury car soon. She lets out a long sigh. It's time to go up the street, a few blocks away.

She pulls a cell phone out of her purse and calls a cab. It takes about ten minutes to get to her. Chantal, annoyed, steps out of the car and slams the door a little too hard causing the side view mirror to fall to the ground, shattering the glass. Chantal curses, stomps her foot in disgust, and jumps into the cab. The driver looks curiously at her fancy clothes and the beater car. She tells him where to go and hums the same French song until they pull into a driveway four blocks away.

The cab drives away as Chantal walks into the Open Door courtyard and sees two men bent over a man lying on the ground. One of them says, "It will be okay." She thinks the man on the ground is sick as the men rub his head. As Chantal gets closer one of the men stomps his booted foot on top of the man's chest. The man on the ground yells in pain. "It will be okay once you pay for giving our stuff to the police!" the man says.

Chantal gasps, the men stand up and turn around to look at her. She realizes they are quite big, with beards and a dangerous look in their eyes. She recognizes the man on the ground as the old man who was kicked out of the grocery store by the manager.

Chantal runs to the door of the shelter yelling, "Help, help, a man is being attacked!"

The two men step away from the old man and he struggles to his feet. Two minutes later, three men run from inside the shelter and Chantal points to the corner of the courtyard. Lee quickly follows and stops at the bottom of the steps. She's on a cordless phone talking to a 911 operator and catches a glimpse of faces as they run along the side of the house.

She instantly recognizes the two brothers that look like twins and who normally eat at Open Door. Lee tells the operator, "I know them, they come to the shelter."

The volunteers run outside to help the old man. Lee's face is flushed as she clutches the phone.

The old man is limping toward the front door. "I'm fine. Leave me alone."

Lee rushes to him. "Please let us help you." She waves the other volunteers away from him. "Just come inside," Lee pleads with the old man.

His face is clearly bruised and a trickle of blood is coming from the side of his mouth. "I don't want to want to talk to any cops. I'm fine."

"I know you had a run-in with the police the other day," Lee says. "Are you in some kind of trouble?"

The old man takes a deep, painful breath. "Miss Lee I didn't do nothing wrong." She gives him a skeptical look. "It's true, just ask the police. I turned in stolen stuff I found near some apartments by the Carter Center. Those brothers stole the stuff and somehow found out what I did."

Lee blinks a couple of times and nods. "I understand now, this all makes sense. I know you don't like talking to people."

She looks him directly in his eyes. "I give you my word that I won't tell the police you're here. Just come inside so we can make sure you're okay."

While Lee gently puts her arm across his shoulder and leads him into the house, a volunteer shows Chantal into Lee's office to wait for her. After she makes sure the old man is okay, Lee goes into the office to thank Chantal. She finds her looking at some brochures on the desk, with her back to the door. She sees the back of her head and thinks the scarf she's wearing is nice.

Lee clears her throat and says, "Thanks so much for helping. It wasn't near lunch time which is why the courtyard was empty. Thank God you came when you did."

Chantal turns around.

Lee's mouth drops open. "Oh my God! She steps closer. "Casey! I thought I would never see you again!"

Chantal answers, "Hi, mother."

Lee cries as she hugs her daughter. Chantal tensely hugs her back and smiles awkwardly. Lee finally steps back and places her hands tenderly on her daughter's shoulders, and looks puzzled. "One of my volunteers said your name was Chantal?"

"I'm sorry, mom, that's the name I go by now. I started using it when I was singing at a nightclub in France." Chantal takes a step back, uncomfortable under her mother's probing gaze.

Lee eyes are open wide with surprise. "Okay, if that's what you prefer."

Chantal rubs the back of her neck and takes another step back. "It is. No one calls me by the other name anymore."

"I see," Lee says quietly. Something is off with her daughter but she can't put her finger on it. She knows that asking her directly won't give her answers. "Well, whatever you call yourself, you're still my daughter and I'm glad you finally came back. I've been so worried about you. Why did you leave without saying goodbye? And you never called or wrote to tell me how you were."

Chantal hangs her head down. "I'm sorry that I put you through that. I will explain everything later."

"We have a lot of catching up to do. But, right now would like you something to eat or drink?"

Chantal sighs longingly and says, "It would be wonderful to have chicken salad with grapes on a baguette, with a side of fresh tomatoes, and..." Her mother adjusts her glasses and looks at her daughter in disbelief. Chantal looks embarrassed and continues haltingly, "Of course, I know this isn't a restaurant. I'm sorry."

"I'll be back with some food." Her mother leaves. Chantal takes a deep breath, relaxes a little and is relieved her mother left the room.

Lee asks some volunteers to fix a sandwich. Then she quickly runs upstairs to the old man. He's resting in the bed that Lee or one of the volunteers uses when they're too tired to drive home. It's in a private room, apart from the group residential area.

Lee stands next to his bed. "How are you feeling?"

"I'm fine, Miss Lee. One of the docs from the clinic is on his way to check me out. Don't think I have any broken bones."

"Good." Lee sits down on the side of his bed, folds her hands together as if she's about to pray. "I just wanted you to know that the woman who called for help is my daughter." She looks around to make sure no one is walking into the room before whispering, "You showed me in that vision that Casey—she calls herself Chantal now—was coming back to me." Lee chokes back tears and dabs her eyes. "I guess it was meant for her to come back to help you as part of her homecoming." She leans over to kiss the old man on the cheek. "Thank you."

Lee leaves. The old man looks surprised as he watches her leave and thinks that he didn't really do anything— it's what was supposed to happen anyway.

Lee brings a sandwich and a Coke to Chantal as the police arrive. They take statements from both of them and Lee tells them the old man has left the shelter. The police confirm that he had turned in items that the brothers stole. "We caught one of the brothers up the street, but the other one is still missing," says the cop.

"Please be on the lookout since both men are wanted for murder," the other cops says as the two men leave.

Chantal shudders. "It doesn't sound like you're safe here, mom. You should go home."

"I'm not scared. God will protect me. Plus, people here need me." She smiles reassuringly. "How did you know I was working here, Casey?" Chantal gives her a sharp look. "Uh—I mean, Chantal. I'll have to get used to saying your new name."

"One of my friends here in Atlanta saw an article that said you were taking the place of the director who died."

Lee is hurt to realize that Chantal had stayed in touch with someone here, but she chose not say anything. Instead, she asks Chantal, "How long did you live in France?"

"Five years," Chantal replies.

"You obviously loved singing there. Did you model, too?"

"Yes," Chantal responds. She doesn't sound enthusiastic and is deliberately giving short answers.

Lee flashes a big smile. "You always have been a good singer. It doesn't surprise me that you were successful. So, are you going back to France?

Chantal shakes her head. "I probably won't go back."

Lee looks puzzled. "Why?"

"It's a long story...but I'm home for good now."

"That's wonderful," Lee says. "I'll have to cook a special dinner to celebrate your homecoming. Then we can go shopping, visit family, work together, take some trips..." Chantal stares at her. Lee laughs, "Oh, let me stop yammering on." She hugs Chantal and caresses the scarf, near her neck. Chantal jumps a little. "That's a pretty scarf. Take off your sunglasses so I can see your beautiful face. I haven't seen you in so long."

Chantal looks startled and moves her mother's hand away. "I need to tell you something, mother."

Lee looks concerned. "What's wrong?"

With her eyes cast downward, Chantal slowly takes off the glasses, loosens the scarf at the neck, then she slips it down to her shoulders. The left side of her cheek, toward the ear is badly burned. The burns extend down past her chin onto her neck. The side of her cheek is a mound of thick flesh and her neck is a jagged formation of webbed skin. It's horrific and unexpected. Lee cries out loudly then covers her mouth. Chantal quickly puts her scarf and sunglasses back on. "Oh sweetheart, oh my God, what happened!?" Lee cries. She steps forward and hugs her daughter.

"There was a fire...I...I" Chantal begins to explain and then cries.

"Shh...shh." Lee rocks her back and forth as if she's a baby. "It's okay, it's okay. Tell me later. All that matters is that you're back."

Chantal cries hard for a long time on her mother's shoulder. She hadn't cried like this in a long time, not even when she first was burned. Lee is grateful that the old man's vision has come true, but not like this, not with her daughter in such an appalling condition. Lee cries as she holds Chantal.

Chapter 18
TIME TO PAY THE PIPER

Gerald and his attorney, Dennis, arrive at the Fulton County courthouse where Valerie is already waiting in the lobby. Gerald and Dennis are walking up the courthouse steps when they spot Tony and his attorney. Tony has his usual smirk planted firmly on his face as he stares hard at Gerald. A shudder goes down Gerald's spine as the dread he's had the last several weeks becomes unbearable.

There's a sound of loud voices and footsteps running up the steps behind Gerald. Dennis tells Gerald to keep walking as he turns around to see what's going on. As Gerald gets to the top of the steps he sees a sea of reporter's faces, with the familiar face of TV news reporter Monica Stewart out in front. Surprisingly, they rush past Gerald and run up to Tony. TV cameras are rolling and other cameras quickly snap pictures with flashbulbs popping. People inside, including Valerie, hurry outside to see what's going on.

"This is Monica Stewart," the news reporter says. "We're here live at the Fulton County courthouse. Atlanta businessman Tony Vitrelli of the Fine Life

Restaurant Group has just been charged with conspiracy and fraud for illegally causing Ernesto Torres and his family to sell their popular Cuban restaurant, and embezzling funds from his family-owned business. The Torres' are suing Vitrelli for two million dollars." She turns to Tony and asks, "What is your response to these charges, Mr. Vitrelli?"

The TV camera zooms in on Tony's shocked face. He looks like a deer in the headlights. His lawyer quickly steps in front of him. "My client has no comment at this time!" Tony nods. Several reporters shout questions as Tony and his lawyer turn away and leave the courthouse.

Monica Stewart continues. "Torres says he hired a private investigator and found out that Vitrelli paid a man to put rats and hazardous material inside their restaurant so they would fail inspection and be forced to close. Vitrelli then bought the property. The private investigator also found out that Vitrelli was embezzling from Fine Life Restaurant Group owned by his father-in-law. We'll have more details on the 6 o'clock news." She finishes and heads inside the courthouse.

"I can't believe it!" Gerald says, staring at the scene that has just unfolded. Dennis tells him to wait inside while he finds Tony's attorney. Gerald sees Valerie in the crowd of people, takes her hand and leads her inside away from the chaos.

Valerie's mind is frozen as she follows him. She's stunned to learn that her former escort client is Tony, Gerald's ex-business partner. She remembers the night that Tony called wanting to see her and bring his business partner over to celebrate their big deal closing—that was Gerald. She realizes that she came much too close to seeing Gerald as a client.

Gerald's lawyer walks up and motions to him. "Wait here, I'll be right back," he tells Valerie. She suddenly feels faint and sits down in a large leather chair in the lobby.

Ten minutes later, Gerald comes back and begins to tell her what Dennis said but she's not listening. "Do you hear me? Baby, it's over. My lawyer just told me that Tony dropped the lawsuit and won't tell the newspaper about my tenant. He can't risk any more of his bad ways being revealed in court or on the news."

"That's great," Valerie says weakly.

Gerald searches her face. "You okay?"

"I am. This is just a big shock. The main thing is that you're okay and that…that guy isn't suing you and going to the press." She hugs Gerald.

Gerald holds her tightly. Valerie is now deeply worried that Gerald might somehow find out about her having been a prostitute. It's a fear she cannot shake.

Chapter 19
FITTING IN

Coming home means different things to different people. For Chantal it doesn't necessarily mean coming home to stay with her mother. She tells Lee that she's staying with friends.

"Chantal, I insist you come home for at least a few days," Lee tells her and Chantal finally relents.

Later that evening, Chantal pulls up to the brick house with green shutters. The yard is neat. Daffodils are near the mailbox and magnolia trees line the driveway.

Lee rushes outside. "Why did you take a cab? I could have picked you up at your friend's house."

"It's not an inconvenience, mother. I'm used to taking cabs and I know how busy you are." Chantal didn't mention that her car had broken down. Lee looks at her strangely as Chantal pays the driver. Then Lee grabs her two bags. "Mom, you don't have to do that. One of those bags is very heavy."

But Lee is already rolling one bag on the ground and has the other bag in hand as they walk to the front door. She smiles. "Sweetie, you know your mama is strong."

Once inside, Lee puts the bags down and hugs her daughter. "Welcome back home!"

"It's good to be back," Chantal says quietly.

"Just relax. I can unpack your bags and run a hot bath for you."

"Mother, please, you don't have to do that."

"But, I want to. I love taking care of you."

"I'm fine with unpacking my own bags. Really, I insist."

There are fresh daffodils in the foyer next to a picture of Jesus. Chantal feels like a visitor in a museum, pieces of memories are perched proudly around every corner, her mother the unknowing curator.

Chantal barely looks at the pictures in the foyer. Lee asks, "Remember when you were a little girl and sang and danced in pageants?"

Chantal slightly nods and reluctantly looks at thin, gold framed pictures with her bright smile matching the twinkling crown and trophy in hand standing on stage. All three of them are in this picture—mother, father, and daughter. Right before Chantal left home her father had a stroke and ended his days in a nursing home.

In the den, blue walls are adorned with pictures of Chantal wearing different crowns and tulle dresses. There are also modeling pictures clipped from local magazines when she modeled dresses and jewelry during her high school years. She is—was—beautiful with gleaming blue eyes, long blond hair, and flawless alabaster skin. Familiarity should have been welcoming, but she's now a stranger visiting a place from a long time ago. The pictures are relics of happier days—cruel reminders of her lost beauty. Chantal just wants to crawl inside herself and cry, and get away from the house as soon as possible. But for now she goes to her old room while Lee begins to cook dinner.

After dinner they talk about Chantal volunteering at Open Door a few days a week. She's quiet. Sensing her sadness, Lee says, "This is a good way for us to spend time together."

Over the next few weeks, Chantal does volunteer work at the shelter. Lee proudly tells everyone how her daughter saved the old man. With each passing day Lee realizes how much Chantal has changed.

"Do you remember how you enjoyed volunteering with me when you were growing up? I thought being here would help you feel better."

"Mom, I enjoy…being here…it's just…just…that…I have different interests now."

Lee frowns. "I understand. Eventually you will get back to your normal self."

Chantal shakes her head. "Mother, your whole life revolves around helping other people and me. You…you smother me. You always have."

Lee looks surprised. "I never meant for you to feel that way, dear. You are my only child."

"I'm not trying to drag up bad memories, but it's been a burden being the only child and knowing that you still silently grieve for my sister."

A pained look comes across Lee's face. "You don't remember when Maggie was killed in that car accident. You were barely three. It's hard for me to forget."

"I know it must have been hard. I always felt I was replacing her and you smothered me."

"I'm sorry. I guess that's why you left without saying goodbye."

"I know you love me. I just need some space. I think I'll cut back to just twice a week at Open Door."

"Whatever works best for you, dear," Lee says and looks at Chantal reflectively. Then she walks away.

The next day Chantal is at Open Door, heading to the kitchen to let Gerald know that a new refrigerator will be delivered tomorrow morning. Chantal enters the kitchen to see Gerald chasing Valerie around the table. Two other volunteers are there. Everyone is laughing hysterically.

Gerald yells to Valerie, "I'll going catch you, you evil witch!"

"No way!" Valerie yells back. Valerie doesn't see Chantal as she runs toward her. Gerald has a spray bottle in his hand and sprays Valerie in the face as she ducks. Some water gets on Chantal's face and scarf. Valerie yells and laughs. "I'm melting, meltinggg!" and purposely drops to the floor at the same time that Chantal shouts angrily, "What are you doing!" She brushes water from her scarf.

Everyone is still laughing and Gerald says, "I'm sorry, I didn't see you. Are you okay?"

Valerie chimes in as she gets off the floor. "I'm sorry, too."

"No, I'm *not* okay. I'm all wet."

Valerie grabs some paper towels off the counter and goes to Chantal. She begins to wipe her off.

Chantal flinches and snatches the paper towels from her. "Do *not* touch me."

Valerie is startled. "I was just trying to help."

Everyone looks at each other uncomfortably as Chantal dabs at her scarf. The two volunteers quietly leave the kitchen.

Gerald looks apologetic. "We were just having fun. Sorry to get you wet." He turns to put away the spray bottle and rolls his eyes.

Chantal wipes herself dry. "I guess I'm okay. As long as it's not some cleaning solution you sprayed, my silk scarf shouldn't have to be replaced."

"Just let me know if it's damaged and I'll be more than happy to replace it for you," Gerald offers.

"I appreciate that," Chantal says with a nod and throws the paper towels away. "My mother says that a refrigerator is being delivered tomorrow and for you be here at ten o'clock."

"I'll be here," Gerald replies as Chantal walks off in a huff.

Valerie and Gerald look at each other. "What's her problem?" Gerald asks.

Valerie looks puzzled. "I guess she didn't want to mess up her Audrey Hepburn scarf."

Gerald thinks for a second. "She sure loves that scarf and sunglasses look. Lee says she's very sensitive to light. But I'm not buying that story. Chantal's in disguise and hiding from Interpol."

Valerie gets a paper towel and wipes her face then opens the dishwasher. "The other volunteers have been saying that, too. Hmm...I don't know."

"Chantal *did* just get back from France. I'm telling you, she's on the run."

"She is strange, but I don't think she's running from the law. Maybe we should feel a little sorry for her."

"Something else is going on, some other secret," Gerald says.

"Maybe you're right," Valerie says as she stacks dishes in the dishwasher. "It's hard to believe that Chantal is Lee's daughter. They're nothing alike." Valerie closes the dishwasher and turns it on.

"Chantal's being here is awkward," Gerald says. "She's not good with office work. The residents don't like her. She can't even make a sandwich."

Valerie folds some dishtowels and starts to sweep the floor. "Well, she doesn't have to do any real work. This is her way of spending time with her mother."

"Okay, okay. I hear you. By the way, did I thank you for being so supportive of me at court?" He comes behind Valerie and hugs her, leaning over to kiss her on the cheek.

"Yes, you did thank me several times," Valerie replies. "But feel free to thank me again." She turns around to kiss him.

Lee clears her throat behind them. "Sorry to interrupt."

Gerald and Valerie suddenly separate, both embarrassed.

Lee chuckles. "You two do so much work here—a little romance never hurt anyone." She looks around the kitchen. "Have you seen Chantal?"

"She came in earlier to tell me about tomorrow's delivery," Gerald replies. "She left a little while ago."

"Well, she's probably around somewhere," Lee says, forcing a smile.

Lee goes to her office to do some paperwork and return a few phone calls. She gets up from her desk and stretches, then heads outside to do her daily six block walk.

Lee nears the tree on the corner when she hears Chantal say loudly, "You promised you would send me some money, what am I supposed to do now!?" She's leaning against the tree talking on her cell phone, wildly waving her hand in the air. "You lied to me. I have no—" She looks up and sees her mother standing there, staring in shock. Chantal quickly hangs up the phone.

"What's wrong, honey?" Lee asks.

Chantal quickly turns away. "Nothing, nothing."

Lee walks toward Chantal. "Why didn't you tell me you're having money problems?"

Chantal turns her back to her mother. "Mom, please don't make me get into this. I have money, it's just that someone owes me and I just told them that I didn't have any money so they would pay sooner than later." She fumbles with the rim of her sunglasses.

Lee looks at her doubtfully. "You know that if you ever need anything, you can always come to me."

Chantal smiles, fidgeting awkwardly from one foot to the other. "I appreciate that, but I don't need any help."

As Lee stands looking at her daughter, not quite sure what to say, voices come from the top of the driveway. They faintly hear Gerald and Valerie saying goodbye. Car doors slam. Gerald drives out, first waving to Lee and Chantal. Valerie follows close behind.

Lee waves goodbye to both of them, then turns back to her daughter and shakes her head. "I was looking for you earlier to see if you wanted to take a walk with me. But, I suppose you have a lot on your mind and I don't want you to feel like I'm *smothering you.* See you later." Chantal watches her mother walk down the driveway out onto the street.

Chantal sighs, fighting back tears. She definitely doesn't want her mother worrying about her. Besides, there's nothing Lee could do to help her anyway. Chantal's problems are very complicated.

Chapter 20
THE RIGHT THING

Gerald reflects on how close he came to losing his business and makes a promise to himself to never let greed take over his life again. Surviving the ordeal with Tony has shown him that the man he was before is no longer the man he wants to be now. He wants to continue on the path of helping people, the one he started by volunteering at Open Door.

Gerald drives to the other side of town to visit the elderly woman whose husband committed suicide. He pulls into the driveway of her small house. Two young children exuberantly chase a puppy in the front yard. A rusty car without wheels sits in the backyard. Before he can get out of the car, the front door bangs open and the old woman pokes her head out. She has on a white apron and holds a pair of tongs in one hand.

She wipes her brow with the back of her hand and frowns when she sees Gerald. She calls the children, "Malachi! Ashley! Go inside and wash your hands. Lunch is almost ready."

One of them says, "Okay, Mo'dear," as they quickly run inside.

Gerald steps out of his car. "What the hell are you doing here!?" she asks as she comes out of the house.

"Mrs. Adams, I'm here to apologize about what happened to your husband," Gerald says softly.

She puts the tongs in the pocket of her apron and looks him up and down. "Hmph! It's a little too late for that, ain't it? Get outta here."

"I know it's been a long time, but I'm sorry for the pain I caused you," Gerald says. He reaches into his pocket, and pulls out an envelope. "And I want to give you this," he says, handing Mrs. Adams the envelope.

She opens it and her eyes widen in surprise as she sees a check inside. "One hundred thousand dollars." She stares at Gerald. "Is this for real?" He nods. "That's a lot of money."

"No amount of money can ever replace your husband. I didn't know that raising the rent put a strain on him and other people renting space in my building. I don't want you to struggle anymore."

Mrs. Adams' eyes fill with tears. "I can't believe this. I never thought you cared."

"But I do," Gerald says, getting teary eyed himself. "I set up a $50,000 scholarship in your husband's name for high school students in your community. And I lowered rental rates back to what it was two years ago before I bought the building."

She claps her hands together. "Hallelujah, my prayers have been answered! Thanks so much. You have no idea what this means to my family and the folks that live 'round here."

Gerald smiles. "I'm just happy to do something good. There's a letter inside with all the information you need, including my phone number. Don't hesitate to call me if you need anything." Gerald turns to leave.

"Wait a minute, wait minute. Don't go off so quick," Mrs. Adams says, then suddenly hugs Gerald tightly. He's surprised when she says, "Stay for lunch. We've got plenty of food. I fried some chicken and baked a squash casserole for my grandkids."

Gerald starts to say no but changes his mind. "That sounds delicious Mrs. Adams, I—"

"Call me Mo'dear, everyone calls me that," she says, taking him by the arm and leading him inside.

"Okay, Mo'dear, you don't have to ask me twice."

The past always has a way of catching up with you if you run away from it. Now, Gerald realizes, he doesn't have to run.

Chapter 21
THE GAME IS WON

Valerie and Gerald are on the floor, laying on cushy throw pillows, sipping red wine and eating organic popcorn in his den.

"Oh, no! That can't be a real word!" Valerie shakes her finger at him. She throws a piece of popcorn at him and it lands in his wine glass.

Gerald looks at the letters spelled on the Scrabble game board: K-I-R-M-E-S-S. He has a mischievous glint in his eye and laughs. "I'm telling you it is." He picks the popcorn out of his wine glass. "Throwing popcorn will not help. I'm still winning."

Valerie throws her hands up in mock disgust. "Stop snickering." She laughs. "Okay, you may be right. What does the word mean?" She reaches into the popcorn bowl and throws some popcorn at his head.

"Challenge me and look it up in the dictionary," he taunts. The popcorns bounce off his head onto the floor.

"No way, I'm not doing that again. I lose points that way."

"Okay, you won't lose any points," Gerald promises. "Kirmess means outdoor fair or festival. I tell you what I'll do since I want you to win. I'll take that word off the board and put down another one that I think you know."

Valerie rolls her eyes. "Hmm."

He takes away all but four letters that spell, K-I-S-S. "I told you, you would know the word." He leans close to Valerie. "That means you win the game."

"Good," Valerie says.

Gerald leans in closer until their noses almost touch. "But...you have to act the word out right now."

They look deeply into each others eyes and kiss. Gerald holds Valerie tightly and runs his fingers through her hair. They bump the Scrabble board and letters fly across the floor. They stop kissing and stare at each other intensely for such a long time that it almost turns into a meditation.

Valerie sharply draws in her breath. His eyes trace her lips and the contours of her cheeks. Her chest is beating so hard she thinks the buttons on her shirt will pop open. Valerie looks down at the scattered letters.

Gerald cups her chin in his hand. His eyes tell her what she already knows. For some strange reason his hand shakes as he takes Valerie's hand and leads her into the bedroom toward a big, four poster bed in the center of the room.

A life-sized nude sculpture of a Greek goddess sits next to the bed.

He kisses Valerie and caresses her back, then steps away to gaze at her. Valerie stands very still. Moonlight peaks through the embroidered silk curtains on the window, streams across her face and heaving chest, and turns her into a beautiful statue of the night. There's newness and uncertainty in her eyes. She trembles. Gerald waits. Then, Valerie undresses slowly, shyly in front of him. He slowly takes off his clothes.

Valerie isn't prepared for the light and gentle touching of his fingers. His flickering fingers are so intense that she cries out in surprise and pleasure. Gerald slowly feels the softness of her skin, inhales the perfume on her neck, and explores her entire body.

Gerald pauses to see Valerie's eyes glowing with desire in the dark. Valerie's nails are in his back as she pushes him forward. He's on top of her, moving quickly inside her. His excitement rises with each movement as if a flame has been ignited within him. Gerald slows down, his belly sliding against hers from their mingled sweat, and kisses Valerie with a passion he's never felt before. Gerald caresses her breasts, licks her neck, savoring how good she tastes and feels. Valerie wraps her legs around him tightly and moans. Her energy feeds him and moves throughout his body. Gerald closes his eyes, feels her breath trickle against his neck as she gasps, and moves with her body. He realizes at that moment that this is the first time he's truly making love to a woman. The sudden revelation startles him. Gerald stops moving and opens his eyes. Valerie's half closed eyes are looking up into his eyes. He gently kisses her, slowly begins to move, and closes his eyes again until they are both exhausted and satisfied.

Afterwards, Valerie cries when he touches her face tenderly. She tries to turn her head away because she's embarrassed. Gerald cradles her face in his hand and kisses away the tears. Valerie turns on her side to slide out of bed. Gerald embraces her, she stiffens, and he spoons behind her, molding the back of her body into his chest and legs. She wants to be as close to him as possible and run away at the same time.

Gerald whispers in her ear, "You aren't going anywhere."

She whispers back, "I just need, need..." Her voice trails off.

Gerald asks, "What?"

Valerie pauses. "Some water."

He chuckles at her lie. "Okay, I'll get you some." He starts to get out of bed.

"No, please don't leave," she whispers breathlessly.

Gerald moves back behind her and kisses her neck. She smells like lavender mixed with his sweat. He puts his hands around her waist. "I didn't think you were thirsty."

Valerie relaxes, smiles, tears up a little and realizes she's in love. Gerald caresses her and kisses her shoulders while they are quiet together, lost in their own thoughts. Gerald hasn't been a good lover until now. He was always a selfish lover. Valerie has shown him what real intimacy is. Valerie had always been a lover without love and now Gerald had changed that by opening her heart, not just her body, to love. Valerie turns over to face him and Gerald pulls her to his chest. The sound of his heartbeat beneath her ear lulls her to sleep.

Gerald drifts to sleep with a smile on his face. A dream quickly winds it way into his slumber.

He's driving down a highway somewhere outside of Atlanta. He sort of recognizes where he is, but doesn't see a sign anywhere. Maybe it's past Monticello. It's not quite dark because there's a sprinkle of pink still nestled amongst the darkening blue of the sky. He drives by a huge expanse of trees and passes a gas station with no sign except for the EBT and cigarettes for sale posters on the front door.

Someone sits in the passenger seat next to him but he can't see who it is. He tries to turn his head to look but can't move it or his chest. He grits his teeth and tries again, but the strain hurts his head. It's feels like his head is in a vice. Only his hands can move as they guide the steering wheel. He sees the fuzzy outline of someone out of the corner of his eye. The person is breathing heavy and mumbling something Gerald can't hear. He tries to ask who the person is but finds he can't speak, either.

Gerald fumbles on the console and presses a button to roll the window down. A soft breeze comes into the car, then a huge gust of wind whips through, shaking the car so hard Gerald is scared he will crash. He stops the car on the side of the highway. The person gets out. Gerald can finally move and gets out of the car. The person disappears.

It's now pitch dark as Gerald walks on the road, looking in the direction of where he thought the person may have gone. When he turns back the car has disappeared too. A clear voice inside his *head says, "Forgive me for not forgiving you." That voice sounds familiar. Gerald says it aloud, "Forgive me for not forgiving you." That voice inside his head is actually his own.*

This startles him and Gerald jumps so hard that he wakes the sleeping Valerie. She sits up and looks at him; his back is to her and she sees that he's sleeping. Valerie watches Gerald as he continues his dream.

Gerald sees lights straight ahead coming from the gas station. He doesn't remember the station being so near. He walks to the entrance and sees the most beautiful flowers: birds of Paradise, orchids, climbing plants, and other exotic flora everywhere, hanging in mid-air where fuel pumps and the front of the building would normally be. Fragrance floats in the air. He touches the flowers.

Valerie lays back down to cradle Gerald while he sleeps.

In his dream, the wind gently blows and the flowers move against him. One of the climbing plants gently touches and massages his back. It feels good and he sighs.

Valerie gently touches Gerald's back while he sleeps and he sighs with delight. His skin feels warm beneath her fingertips. As she strokes him, she feels energy coming from him into her hand. It's strange, she thinks, as if it's another person that she's touching and not Gerald. The energy gets stronger and stronger as she continues to touch him. Her hand begins to touch something rough at his neck. She can feel holes and the collar to a jacket.

Valerie sits up abruptly, wondering how that can be since Gerald is naked. She pulls her hand away and sees the outline of someone different lying next to her. From the light coming in the window, she can see a head with a different shaped head than Gerald's, with very thick hair. She can't tell who it is. Then a thought seeps into her mind: the old man! Valerie gasps. She looks and it's Gerald again. She blinks several times to make sure. It's still him. There's no more jacket, no more different shaped head. She rubs her hands on the sheet, then timidly touches him again. The energy isn't there anymore. Why would she be feeling and seeing the old man from the shelter?

While the plants continue to stroke Gerald in the dream, the old man walks out of nowhere and looks at Gerald. His face lightly glows in the moonlight. Gerald stares back at him in disbelief. "What are you doing here?"

Gerald wakes up with a start. Valerie hears him ask, "What are you doing here?" Gerald moves away from her stroking hands, fully waking up.

She answers, "I'm here because we fell asleep making...love," Valerie replies. "You were dreaming." Valerie gives him a puzzled look.

Gerald turns toward her and says drowsily, "Sorry to wake you, baby."

Valerie looks at him closely. He looks fine. "It's okay. I was on my way to the bathroom."

Valerie gets up and goes into the bathroom. She wonders if Gerald was talking to the old man in his dream. Something strange, something very strange, is definitely going on.

While Valerie is in the bathroom, Gerald wonders why she looked at him so confused. He wonders why he dreamed of the old man again. Nothing is making sense anymore.

Chapter 22
ART AT MARY MAC'S

Several busy days at Trendz boutique keeps Valerie and Gerald from seeing each other after their night filled with lovemaking and a dream. They talk on the phone in soft voices and but no mention is made about the significance of that night. It's as if words will break the love spell. But Valerie can't help remembering the feeling of the old man's energy when she touched Gerald that night. She almost says something about it on the phone each time they talk but then changes her mind. She doesn't want him to think she's crazy.

Valerie comes to Open Door one day just as Gerald is helping Lee load up a passenger van with art painted by some of the shelter's residents. They're going to sell the paintings for a fundraiser. Valerie walks toward the van as Gerald wraps a blanket around a big piece of art.

"Valerie, you're just in time," Lee says. "The art is ready to be delivered. You coming with us?" Gerald comes over to hug and kiss Valerie.

"Of course I'm coming." She smiles as Lee goes back inside. Valerie turns to Gerald. "I got off work earlier today and I wanted to see you."

"I wanted to see you, too." He takes Valerie's hand. "Take a look at what Ralph painted."

Valerie stares at the painting. It has a dark and light blue sky filled with streaks of red. A man floats out of the sky, a face with no mouth or nose. It is indefinable and blurry, except for piercing blue eyes. Haunting sadness mixed with anger lay in the depths of those eyes. A bloody hand clutches the lapels together of a tattered long, gray coat. On his feet are worn black work boots, the lace is missing from one, while the other lace dangles loose, blown to the side. It is a beautiful and striking painting.

Valerie opens a folder next to it to read the description: God is a Homeless Man by Ralph Murphy. "Wow, this is amazing. Ralph's talents are wasted as a sandwich maker."

"Yes, he's quite talented," Gerald sys with a nod. They wrap the rest of the art.

After a few more minutes of packing, Valerie finally says, "Remember the other night when you woke from dreaming?"

"Unh-huh."

She looks at him hesitantly. "I know this is going to sound silly...did you dream about the old man with the green suitcase?"

Gerald stops wrapping and stares at Valerie.

Inside the shelter, with Chantal's help, Lee is gathering a few smaller pieces of art from the office. "I'm so happy you're going with me. You always liked art. I remember when we painted pictures of the flowers in the backyard."

Chantal looks thoughtful and smiles. "I remember that."

Lee smiles. "You were good. Remember that art dealer you dated for awhile? He was trying to get you to start painting again. I actually thought you would marry him."

"I almost forgot about him. He wasn't exactly my type. A bit too boring." She picks up a piece of art leaning on the bookcase. "Do you need to take this one?"

"Yes," Lee says and Chantal begins to wrap it up. "There's someone out there for you; you'll get married someday."

Chantal chuckles sarcastically. "I don't think so, mother. It's not like I'm a raving beauty anymore. Anyway, I already have been m—" She catches herself, then continues, "I've been married before, so I haven't missed out on anything."

Lee looks shocked and adjusts her glasses. "Well." She's quiet for a few moments. "I guess there're a lot of things I don't know about."

Chantal regrets letting the truth slip out. "I'm sorry. But, don't feel bad about something that has already happened."

Lee looks hurt. "I know you didn't mean to tell me."

Chantal feels bad. "It's not that I'm hiding anything. I wasn't even married that long—only a few months. I don't want to talk about him—there are too many bad memories."

Lee smiles at her daughter. "Well, I'm not going to pry anymore."

Lee and Chantal gather the art and head to the van. They hear Valerie and Gerald talking.

"I'm telling you it was strange, Gerald, but it was the old man with the green suitcase."

Gerald scratches his head, bends over to pick up a piece of art and places it inside the van. "I'm sure it was nothing; you were just sleepy."

Chantal notices a puzzled look come over Lee's face as Valerie and Gerald turn to see them walking up to the van. Lee stumbles over her words, "Is everything ready?"

"Just finished. I can drive if you like," Gerald says as Lee, Chantal and Valerie climb into the van.

Gerald drives as Lee directs him to Emerging Art Scene, a well-known gallery in Castleberry. She figures the paintings will sell for a high amount there, and the gallery offered to do a special exhibition to raise money for the shelter.

Then they drop some smaller pieces of art at a couple of coffeehouses in Decatur that are holding art events.

On the way back to Open Door, Valerie asks Lee, "How many residents made art?"

Lee is sitting in the back next to Chantal. "This year, thirty residents participated. They really enjoyed it. It takes their mind off their problems."

"Ralph's piece is unique," Gerald says. "I may buy it."

Chantal nods. "Yes, that's a very interesting piece."

Valerie turns to Lee. "Did the old man with the green suitcase paint anything?"

"No he didn't," Lee responds. "But, I didn't expect him to."

"I bet he would paint something interesting since he's so mysterious," Valerie says.

There's a long silence as Gerald and Lee both give Valerie a strange, questioning look. Valerie looks at Gerald and then at Lee sitting behind her.

Chantal wonders what's going on and breaks the awkward silence. "Do you know him very well, mother?"

"No, I don't, dear." Lee pauses. "He doesn't really talk much to anyone."

Chantal senses her mother is being evasive.

Valerie points to the corner of the van, near Chantal's purse where there are two small pieces of art. "Where do these go?"

Lee looks. "Gosh, we forgot these two. They go to Mary Mac's restaurant up the street. Gerald, can you please turn around so I can drop theme off?"

"No problem." Gerald turns around at the next intersection.

"I'll deliver them real quick," Valerie offers.

"Thanks, Valerie, my feet can use the rest," Lee says with smile.

Gerald turns on Myrtle Street and parks in the back of the restaurant. The smell of home made biscuits and fried chicken wafts into the van. Everyone's noses turn toward the scent and remark on how good it smells—except for Chantal, who wrinkles her nose in disgust.

"I haven't eaten here in awhile," Gerald says. "I'd love some fried chicken and peach cobbler. Does anyone else want something? My treat."

Valerie and Lee smile and say yes simultaneously, while Chantal declines.

Valerie writes down Gerald's and Lee's order and Gerald gives her some money. As she leaves she asks Chantal, "Are you sure you don't want anything?"

"No, thank you, I don't like Southern food."

Lee looks surprised. "But you used to eat it all the time."

Everyone looks at Chantal. She caresses her scarf at the neck. "That was a long time ago, mother."

Lee purses her lips. "Yes, I forgot you prefer French food." She pats her daughter's leg. "Perhaps later next week the two of us can go to that French restaurant, Anis."

"That sounds nice, mother." Chantal looks at everyone dismissively, then digs into her purse and pulls out her cell phone to check her voicemail.

Valerie goes inside, places the order and gives the manager the small pieces of art. The restaurant isn't fancy but is frequented by quite a lot of celebrities indicated by the photos that line the walls.

Valerie decides to take a few photographs of the art and realizes she left her phone in the van. She walks outside to get it and to the left of the restaurant, sees the old man at the opposite corner on Penn Avenue. His back is to her. She stops dead in her tracks and swallows hard. She wants to approach him. But, will she say, "*Excuse me, I saw you in my boyfriend's bed when we were half asleep; were you actually there*?" Valerie chuckles to herself. No, not a good idea. Maybe some things are meant to remain a mystery, some questions left unanswered.

Chapter 23
TELL THE TRUTH

The longer Valerie stands staring at the old man the more she cannot resist the urge to ask him. But, ask him what? Just then the old man picks up his suitcase and turns the corner. Valerie goes after him.

The old man looks back, sees her and keeps walking.

Valerie keeps walking, too.

He walks a little more then stops and turns to her. "Stop following me."

Valerie fidgets from one foot to the other. "I'm not...following you. Lee brought us here to deliver art to Mary Mac's."

He asks sarcastically, "Am *I* Mary Mac's, hmm?"

"No, you're not."

"Then, go away!"

The old man walks away and goes into an alley behind a dialysis center with graffiti on the back wall near the fence. There's nothing back there except for trash and a few strolling stray cats. As Valerie follows him she begins to feel that same energy when she touched Gerald the other night in bed. He stops, kicks a broken beer bottle on the ground, sets his green suitcase down and sits on top of it. The old man looks at her as if he's waiting for something and shakes his head. Valerie feels the energy building up in her head, chest, and stomach. Her head feels as though a heavy weight is inside it and her stomach feels queasy.

She grabs her head and her stomach in fear. "What's happening?"

The old man grumbles, "I should've known."

The top of the suitcase begins to shake slightly until it shakes so hard he has to stand up so he won't fall off. He lets out an exasperated sigh. The old man holds his face in his hands and his entire face moves. He looks up and his wrinkles are quivering. The suitcase bounces across the ground flecking up dirt and gravel. Pieces of gravel bounce off the old man's chest. Dirt flies across Valerie's face and arms.

The old man's arms and chest begin to shake and he folds his arms into his chest. Valerie's mouth opens wide with surprise. He steps closer to her and she can feel energy pouring out of him in thick waves toward her. He opens his arms wide like a minister leading a prayer in church and closes his eyes tight. The bouncing suitcase shoots energy toward Valerie and propels her toward the old man.

Valerie gasps. The old man lowers his arms and extends his gnarled hands to her.

"Take my hands." His voice sounds like he's at the far end of a tunnel. Valerie sees his eyes are still closed and hesitates. He repeats again insistently, "Take my hands."

Valerie puts her hands into his. Immediately the energy passes from his hands to hers. It presses and folds her in a cocoon of warmth. She closes her eyes and loses track of time.

Then Valerie opens her eyes. The old man is still in a trance-like state. She turns and releases one of her hands from his and sees the suitcase has stopped moving. Pieces of gravel are suspended in air forming a perfect square filled entirely with white space. The area on either side of the square, the brick buildings and ground where she stood are still there. It was as if the square had dropped into that part of the outside.

The square gets a little darker. Images form and the outline of furniture fill quickly with color and detail. A cream colored chair and sofa become visible until Valerie realizes that she's looking at the living room inside her apartment. Her mother is sitting on her couch going through Valerie's purse, looking over her shoulder like she doesn't want to be seen, and then quickly stuffs two hundred dollars into her bra. Valerie walks into the room with a soft drink and hands it to her mother.

The scene suddenly goes away and Valerie sees herself counting and recounting the money, looking puzzled. There's a knock on the door and her client Jeff comes in. What she's seeing happened months ago in her apartment on the day Tony wanted to see her but she saw Jeff instead. Now she knows what happened to her rent money. Her own mother had stolen part of it.

The square turns white again. Then, Valerie sees herself in her bed with Tony, looking up at the ceiling, silently crying. She remembers that horrible night and starts to cry.

The old man says, "Don't hide your secret from Gerald anymore."

"But I will lose him." She wipes tears from her face.

"You must tell him the truth," the old man says gently.

She turns back to the square and sees more images forming. She's sitting at a table with her mother, whose hair is pulled back in a neat ponytail. She's

looking down at a cup of coffee. Then she looks up with a serious expression.
Valerie has a deep scowl on her face and yells at her mother, "It wasn't supposed to be this way!" Then suddenly, the gravel suspended in air crashes down to the ground breaking the square formation.

The vision immediately stops. Valerie is stunned. She looks at the old man. His eyes are open and he looks pale and tired. The old man walks over to grab his suitcase.

She stammers, "How can you, how can you...?"

He turns to leave. "I don't know. It's the power that knows."

"Please don't tell Gerald." She doesn't think he will say anything but isn't sure.

"It's not for me to tell," he says wearily. "You know what to do."

The old man walks away and goes up the street. A tall, big man standing in the shadow of a tree does a double-take after seeing the old man and quickly walks away.

Valerie leans against the building and cries so hard that her cheek chafes against the brick. She desperately doesn't want to lose Gerald, but hates having this horrible secret. And, she can't believe that her mother stole money from her.

Valerie is in a daze as she brushes off the dirt and walks back into the restaurant to pick up the food. Valerie gives the woman at the counter the order while she goes to the bathroom. As Valerie walks away she hears a waitress asking the woman, "I'm thinking about dying my hair red. Do you think I'll look good as a redhead?" She looks back at the gray-haired waitress, whose question makes her remember something from long ago. Valerie goes into the bathroom and runs cold water, staring vacantly into the mirror.

Valerie finishes scrubbing the carpet, the grape juice didn't come out completely. She knows her mother will be upset about it. She heads to the kitchen to clean it before tackling the rest of the house. Valerie picks up dirty plates and pots, adding them to the sink full of dishes. There's a knock on the door. Valerie stops moving and tries to be very quiet.

A female's voice says, "Hello? Hello." Valerie cringes. It's Ms. Waites, a nosy neighbor from next door. "I know you're in there, Valerie. Please open the door."

Valerie rolls her eyes, dries her hands and cracks open the door. Ms. Waites is peering in the crack at Valerie, her thick bifocals almost touch the door. Her red hair is pinned up in bun, with bangs in the front, tendrils of gray curl over her ears. She has on matching bright red lipstick. She once told Valerie's mother that Lucille Ball was her favorite actress and that's why she had been dying her hair red for years. Valerie thinks she looks more like a clown than bearing any resemblance to Lucille Ball.

Ms. Waites says, "I was just stopping by to see how everything is."

"We're fine. Mom's not here right now." Ms. Waites puts her foot in the door.

"I know. I saw her leave in a hurry a few minutes ago."

Ms. Waites pushes the door in and Valerie stumbles back, trying not to lose her balance. Ms. Waites steps inside and looks around at the dirty kitchen.

She gasps loudly. "Ohmygoodness, ohmygoodness, ohmygoodnes! Something told me your mother was off her medication again."

Valerie quickly says, "No, I did this. Look I'm cleaning it up right now."

Ms. Waites looks sadly at her. "Dear, you don't have to lie. I know how your mother is when she gets in one of her fits."

Valerie bursts into tears, burying her face in her hands.

"Please don't cry. You won't get in trouble." Ms. Waites puts her arm around Valerie and pats her back.

"She's off her medication,' Valerie acknowledges. "Please don't tell anyone. I have to take care of her when she comes back. She'll be gone for days. I don't want them to take her away!"

"It'll be okay," Ms. Waites says, still holding and consoling Valerie. "I didn't know you were by yourself. You can stay with me. I'll get your mother help." She walks to the sink, turns on the faucet and fills a glass with water. "Stop crying, dear. Drink this." She hands Valerie the glass of water. "Let me call someone. Then I'll clean up and cook you something to eat. I'm sure you're hungry."

The sound of the running faucet snaps Valerie back to the present. She splashes cold water on her face, dries off with a paper towel and smiles at herself in the mirror. She doesn't want anyone to know anything is wrong.

When she gets back to the van with the food order, she apologizes for taking so long. Chantal is busy checking her voicemail. She listens to a man's voice with a French accent: "I got your messages. Regrettably, I have to break my promise. I won't be sending you any more money. I'm with someone else now.

Not to be cruel, but it's not my fault about the fire. Au revoir, Chantal." Chantal sighs and adjusts her sunglasses.

Gerald smiles. "Oooh, that fried chicken smells great." He guns the engine and drives the van out into the street traffic.

The tall man that was in the shadow of the tree, walks to where he last saw the old man. He's scowling so hard that his thick eyebrows are scrunched together in a massive clump above his eyes. His grits his teeth in anger and strokes his long beard. Now that the police have his brother in jail for murder it's up to him to finish off the old man.

Chapter 24
OUT IN THE OPEN, PT.1

Tonight it's chilly outside as Valerie walks into Gerald's house. He smiles and hands her a glass of red wine. Valerie takes the wine as he shuts the door.

Valerie shudders and rubs her arm as they walk into the den. An ESPN sports show is on TV. "I should have worn a jacket, it's starting to get cool at night now."

"Well, that's why I'm here," Gerald says. "To keep you warm." He hugs and kisses Valerie. "Better?"

"Much," she says.

Valerie sits down, picks up the remote and turns off the TV. "Gerald, something strange happened today."

Gerald eyes her curiously. "Uh-oh, what happened?" He sits down next to Valerie and pours some wine into his glass.

"Well...it's about the old man," Valerie replies.

"Oh." Gerald gets up and walks in front of the fireplace. He avoids looking directly at her.

Valerie watches him carefully. "I know that he gave you a vision."

Gerald raises his eyebrows in surprise.

"As a matter of fact, he gave me a vision today," Valerie says.

Gerald puts his wine down on the mantle behind him. "Damn, really?"

Valerie nods.

"I can't believe it," Gerald says, genuinely shocked.

"Why didn't you tell me?" Valerie asks.

Gerald scratches his chin. "Let's see...I get a vision from an old man, tell you what happened. Probably you'd think I was crazy."

Valerie laughs. "You're right."

Gerald walks closer to her. "It is pretty out there, along with alien abductions and all of that."

"What did he show you, Gerald?"

"You won't believe it, but his vision showed that my business partner Tony was going bankrupt before I found out later." Gerald wisely decides to not tell her about the first vision he received about marrying Christy.

"Wow, that's some gift he has."

"What did he show you?"

Valerie hesitates. "He showed me and my mother arguing. I don't see how that predicts anything since that happens a lot."

"Well, maybe what he showed you signifies the beginning of solving your problem with her. And what's the problem?"

Valerie shrugs. "My mother has been an absent parent for long periods of time. It got worse when my dad died."

"I didn't know that, baby," Gerald says. "Was she an alcoholic or on drugs?"

"No, she wasn't...it was just hard for her to stay in one place after my dad died. I think she was trying to find her way back to him, even though he was dead. Mom couldn't get over the pain of losing him." Valerie wasn't actually lying to Gerald since this is what she actually thought.

"I'm sorry you had to go through all that growing up."

"It wasn't too bad." *Yes, it was.*

"Well, take the vision as something positive," Gerald says.

Valerie thinks about what the old man told her to do and shakes her head. "I'll try to. I also think maybe the old man showed Lee a vision, judging by how she reacted when I asked her questions about him."

Gerald looks thoughtful. "I noticed that too. I think you're right. Let's not question her about it though." Gerald pauses and looks at Valerie. "I wonder why we've all been shown things by the old man and why we're all connected to each other at the shelter."

Valerie tips her head to the side. "Yes, the shelter is where it all began." Her mind drifts away for a few minutes.

Valerie sniffles a little, having cried on the drive over to Open Door. Her eyes are puffy. She dabs at them with a tissue that Ms. Waites hands her. They're in the office of the shelter. A bible is open on top of the desk and a picture of Jesus with hands folded in prayer, hangs on the wall behind the desk.

Ms. Waites sits next to her mother and holds her hand. She was baking cookies with Valerie when the shelter called, and the two of them rushed over to Open Door.

Her mother's hair is wildly piled on her head, like tumbleweed on a prairie range. She's rocking back and forth, mumbling all sorts of things, saying "damn" and "shit" in between talking about a hurricane that happened down the street and that she's sorry for losing her purse.

Noticing Valerie for the first time her mother says in a cracked voice that matches her lips, "Baby, I'm so sorry. I missed your chorus performance at school."

"It's okay, mom."

Ms. Dyer, who runs Open Door walks in. "I'm glad we finally found out who she

*was so we could contact you. You must
have been worried sick."*

*Ms. Waites smiles at Ms. Dyer. "Yes
we were. Thanks for taking care of June."*

*"We found her wandering the streets.
I'm glad we got to her before she got hurt.
Sorry we don't take residents in her
condition."*

*"I understand, you don't have to
apologize," Ms. Waites says.*

*Ms. Dyer looks at Valerie
sympathetically. "I just talked to Grady
Hospital and they say they have a bed
available. They're sending an ambulance
now to pick her up."*

*Valerie hugs her mother, rocking back
and forth with her until the ambulance
arrives. Her blouse smells like old
cigarettes and mothballs. She knows it
will be a long time until she can see her
again. No matter how many years later
Valerie will still remember that smell.*

Gerald breaks into her thoughts.
"Yes, I'm happy I volunteered at Open
Door. If it hadn't been for that, I'd never
have met you."

Valerie smiles. Gerald kisses her and
she shudders.

Gerald rubs her arms and whispers,
"Are you still cold?"

She lowers her eyelashes coyly. "Yes."

He says, "Well, let's do something about that."

Valerie giggles. They kiss and move slowly toward the couch. As he gently lowers Valerie to the cushions, kissing her all the while, she wonders when or if she'll tell him about her past life as a prostitute, and Gerald wonders why he, Valerie, and Lee all have seen visions from the old man. But Gerald forgets all that as they sink deeper into the couch.

Chapter 25
OUT IN THE OPEN, PT.2

Back at the shelter, Chantal and her mother argue, something that Lee rarely does. Lee wants to drive Chantal to her friend's house instead of her taking a cab as she usually does. But Chantal is anxious to get away from her mother, and has to get some things straight inside her head.

Chantal starts to call the cab company. Lee says, "Please put away the phone. It's bad enough you don't want to stay at home. Why won't you let me at least drive you? Why are you being so secretive?"

Chantal hangs up. "I'm not, I just need my space. You're smothering me again!"

"Something is going on. First with the phone call I overheard the other day and now you're upset after listening to your voicemail today."

Chantal glares at her mother and sniffs.

"Don't tell me you're not," Lee says, raising her voice.

Chantal rubs the top of her head, adjusting her scarf lower onto her forehead. She says quietly, "Everything is fine."

Lee slowly shakes her head. "I don't believe that. At least tell me who the friend is that you're staying with."

Chantal sighs. "I'm staying with Melanie."

Lee looks relieved. "Your old college roommate—I remember her, she's a nice girl."

Chantal gets the cell phone out of her purse and calls the cab. She hugs her mother. "I'm sorry for yelling. I know how much you hate that. I'm just a little tired. I'll call you when I get to Melanie's."

Lee smiles. "I just want to make sure you're okay. I need to do a few things here before I go home. I'll talk to you later."

Lee walks away while Chantal waits for the cab. She goes into her office to grab her purse. Lee peeks around the corner to make sure Chantal is still up front, then heads to the parking lot. She gets into her car and waits until she sees a yellow cab pull into the front driveway, then she starts the car. As soon as the cab pulls away, Lee follows.

Chantal tells the driver where to go. He pulls onto the street and she sees the old man walking down the street swinging his green suitcase. She looks at him curiously, remembering how Gerald and her mother reacted to him yesterday.

Chantal's mind scrambles to make sense of the voicemail from earlier that day. She can't believe that David has gone back on his promise to help her. They had dated for two years. He had always taken care of her and even had bought the apartment in Paris. Of course, Chantal realizes his breaking off with her was to be expected, given the way she now looks.

Chantal has no idea what to do now that David isn't her safety net. She had planned on using part of the money from him to pay for the expensive plastic surgery she so badly needs. Chantal remembers that fateful night when her world changed.

It's summertime, Chantal is with David and some friends at Castel Beach in Nice, France. The wind blows through his dark hair. He smiles. A lock of hair brushes past his gray eyes that twinkle at her mischievously.

He says, "Darling don't be that way, it will be fun."

Sylvie and Bernard nod in agreement. They had come down from Paris to meet her and David.

Chantal had just gotten back from a two day photo shoot in Italy that wore her out. They want to go swimming but she doesn't. She looks with irritation at the crowded beach.

"You know I hate it when the damn American tourists are everywhere," she says derisively.

And they were everywhere, as plentiful as the pebbles that filled the beach. Chantal wanted to go out on David's boat.

David kisses Chantal and twirls her around. She melts in his arms. He is so charming and good looking.

He laughs. "You forget that you are a damn American. Let's go for a swim."

Sylvie and Bernard laugh. Chantal finally says reluctantly, "Yes...je suis Amèricain...unfortunately. But, okay, if you insist, mon chèri, then we will go swimming."

At the beach they swim playfully in the clear blue water like dolphins for an hour until hunger fixates inside their bellies. David owns a popular restaurant near the beach and they eat there. David likes to party as much as he likes running his various businesses. He promptly orders wine and champagne for dinner, and two hours later they stumble drunkenly onto his boat laughing, drinking, and smoking cigarettes. Bernard suggests they go dancing at a discothèque and everyone agrees to it. Chantal goes into the cabin to freshen up and change clothes. She puts a glass of champagne down on a table, trips over a chair and falls on the floor. She giggles, gets up and looks at herself in the mirror. Then she takes makeup, hairspray, and a brush out of a drawer. Chantal brushes her hair, then sprays it.

Sylvie comes in and closes the door. "Ohh, let me help you get ready."

Sylvie puts her cigarette down on the side of the table, picks up the hairspray and wildly sprays, saturating Chantal's hair and face, waving her arms like she's conducting a symphony. Then Sylvie sprays her own dark brown hair, pulling it all over her head and spinning around. Chantal begins to spin around, too.

They two fall to the floor, drunk, dizzy and giddy.

Chantal wipes at her eye already sticky from the hairspray. "Heyyy, my eye. I'm wet, but we're not swimming."

They get up and hug each other as they both break into peals of laughter, looking in the mirror at their messy birds nest of hairdos.

There's a knock at the door. Bernard asks, "Are you two ready?"

Sylvie answers, "Almost."

Chantal drinks more champagne, can hardly stand and holds the back of the chair. She tells Sylvie, "Give me a minute."

"Okay, let me get something else to drink." Sylvie stumbles out of the cabin and closes the door.

Chantal drinks the rest of the champagne. She giggles, kisses the mirror, plops down in the chair, and passes out on the table on top of Sylvie's lit cigarette. The left side of Chantal's hair catches fire quickly. Then the left side of her face burns, along with her dress. Chantal comes to, feels heat on her head and jumps from the chair.

Outside on the deck, David sniffs the air. "Is someone cooking something?"

Sylvie and Bernard smell it, too. Sylvie walks toward the cabin and sees smoke rising from underneath the door. "It's coming from the cabin!" she yells as they hear Chantal scream.

They run in and find Chantal lying on the floor, beating at flames on her head and dress. The fire has spread to the table and wall. Sylvie screams and David and Bernard quickly pull Chantal outside the cabin. Bernard runs off. David quickly takes off his shirt to cover her and stop the flames. Bernard rushes back with bottles of water and pours them over her. He runs off to take care of the fire still going in the cabin.

Chantal is not on fire anymore but it's too late. The left side of hair is all gone, *and the left side of her face is pale white, charred, outlined in jagged red lines. Sylvie cradles her, sobbing uncontrollably while David goes for help.*

Later, in the hospital Chantal wakes up alone with only scattered memories of what happened and excruciating pain to keep her company. David wasn't there. Where is he? Where is David? Then she asks that aloud. The nurse explains that he wasn't there, and tells her what happened. Chantal feels her face and the bandages. She wants to take it off to see. The nurse explains that the bandages can't be removed yet to minimize infection and a skin graft needs to be done. When Chantal is finally given a mirror to see herself, she drops it. It shatters, the chards of glass crashing to floor. That was her new life, shattered, changed forever.

Chantal arrives at her destination, wiping tears away from underneath her sunglasses. She pays the driver and walks to the door.

As she fumbles in her purse for the key, a voice behind her asks, "Why on earth are you living here?"

Startled, Chantal turns around to see the shocked look on her mother's face. She's speechless. Lee looks at the parking lot, riddled with trash, used condoms, crack drug pipes, and broken beer bottles. People are milling about in the parking lot, leaning into open windows of cars. Women in short skirts and greasy makeup are walking up the street, eyeballing cars that are slowing down.

Chantal opens the door. "We can't stand out here; come in."

Lee follows Chantal inside the hotel room. A stale smell immediately hits her nose as she walks in. Chantal turns on the light. The walls are scuffed and filled with holes.

"Answer me, why are staying in this horrible hotel?" Lee demands.

Chantal sits on the bed and it squeaks loudly under her weight. "Mother, I didn't want you to worry. I'm...having some temporary money problems."

Lee shakes her head. "I knew it. There's no reason to hide it from me."

Chantal slips her high-heels off. "I've been away for so long and had no contact with you and now here I am coming back with money problems."

"That doesn't matter; you're my daughter," Lee scolds. "You can always stay with me. You certainly can't stay in this dump."

"Mother, there're too many memories at your house—home, that make me want to just crawl away and die— memories of what I was. And I simply can't make that go away."

Lee wrings her hands. "At least tell me what happened to your money? How did the accident happen?"

Chantal turns away. Lee looks at her downcast face and feels her angst wrapped tight around her like a blanket. Her heart breaks for Chantal. Lee wishes she could take away her pain and make things right, but senses that only God can help her daughter.

She sits down next to her and holds her for a long time. Lee bows her head and prays silently while Chantal holds back tears.

Finally Chantal lifts up her head. "Mother, everything will be fine. I won't be at this place for long."

"I hope so. But you know I'll worry and keep checking on you."

Chantal nods and quietly says, "I need you to go now."

Lee looks at her daughter and nods in response. She gets up, walks to the door, and as she opens it, looks at Chantal for several lingering minutes. "I love you."

"I love you, too," Chantal responds.

Lee walks out and gets into her car. She slowly drives home, crying the whole way.

Chapter 26
YOU ARE...

Business deals no longer consume Gerald's life now. And doing bad business is a thing of the past. There's a balance that hadn't been there before. He feels a sense of freedom and contentment—something he's never known. Volunteering at the shelter is now an important part of his life, part of his regular routine, much like his morning ritual of drinking a cup of Turkish coffee. If you had told him last year that his life would be this way, he would have laughed. Sometimes the things that happen unexpectedly are the best ones.

Lee had asked Gerald to bring in supplies for the foot clinic at the shelter. He came back with toe nail clippers, corn pads, and Epsom salts.

Gerald brought everything to a room that was set up like a podiatrist's office. All the items had been donated by the widow of deceased foot doctor in the area. A reclining patient chair had a movable foot rest. And there was a small circular backless chair on wheels for the doctor to sit on, next to a tall floor light and cabinets.

A shuffling at the door catches Gerald's attention. He sees the old man limping in. They look at each other in surprise. The old man is clutching his suitcase under one arm.

He's trying to decide if he should stay or go. "Where's the doc?"

Gerald gestures toward a chair. "Doctor Edwards won't be here for another half hour. Take your shoe off."

The old man sits down reluctantly and slowly takes off his tennis shoe. The bottom of the shoe is worn so thin there are holes in it.

The old man takes off his sock, winces and grunts. "Hmph. It's bad."

The bottom of his foot is rough and cracked with numerous raw blisters on the heel and instep.

Gerald goes to the sink and runs some warm water in a foot tub and pours in some antiseptic soap. "Take off your other shoe and sock. You need to wash your feet and soak in some Epsom salts until he gets here."

Gerald places the pan next to the old man's feet. "I see you know how to doctor, thanks."

Gerald looks at the old man's shoes. "What size do you wear?"

"Eleven."

"I don't think we have that size," Gerald says. "If we don't, I'll go buy some for you. You definitely can't walk around in those. Let me go check." He leaves the clinic.

Gerald comes back with a pair of clean socks. "They didn't have your size, so while you soak I'll get you another pair."

The old man looks surprised. "That's nice of you, thanks."

Gerald goes to the sink and runs some warm water. He fills another foot tub with water and Epsom salts. As he does so, the old man's feet begin to tingle. The tingling sensation moves up his legs, then to his chest, arms and hands. Gerald turns around with the foot tub and sees that the old man is shaking all over and emanating an energy so strong that there's a slight buzzing sound. Gerald drops the foot tub and water splashes all over him and the floor. He walks toward the old man expectantly. Expecting something. And he's not scared. He wants this encounter with the old man again. The old man has a slight smirk on his face as if he can hear what Gerald's thinking.

"What do you have to show me?" Gerald says quietly.

The old man shrugs as he feels his face shaking, his wrinkles trembling with answers to Gerald's questions. Energy builds more and more in the pit of his stomach like a volcano, and cascades into his arms and hands. He can't stand, he's stuck in the chair. The old man's hands are heavy. He can't move them from his lap. "Take my hands."

Gerald bends down to take his hands and is immediately brought to his knees in front of the old man, his feet still soaking. The old man's hands are heavy as anvils and grip Gerald so tightly it feels like his hands are inside steel pipes.

Gerald closes his eyes and the old man's grip lessens. The old man's energy seeps slowly into him, like water pouring into a cup.

A baby cries and Gerald opens his eyes. The sound is coming from behind him at the sink. He tries to turn but the old man's grip is still tight. The old man stares blankly at Gerald, but doesn't see him. He's in a trance. Finally, the old man lets his hands go and Gerald gets up and turns around. The room darkens and Gerald barely sees a woman in a long blue nightgown standing near the sink, her back to him. It's not the same sink that's in the clinic. Gerald is standing in someone else's kitchen.

The woman jostles a fussy baby over her shoulder. "There, there now."

She takes a baby bottle and a white towel off a yellow Formica table. She turns around and Gerald sees her frowning face clearly. It's his mother when she was a young woman.

"Really, you made too much noise coming in late; he was almost asleep."

She puts the bottle in the sink. Gerald wonders who she's talking to. A faint voice in the background responds but he can't hear what is said. Gerald steps closer, remembers the baby's chubby cheeks and patch of dark hair on top of its head, and realizes the baby on her shoulder is him. He reaches out to touch his mother and his hand passes through empty air. She smells likes baby powder and perfume. Probably the baby powder smell is coming from the baby—him. Gerald laughs. Her auburn hair is shiny like it has been freshly washed.

She drops the towel on the linoleum floor. "It won't take long to get Gerald to sleep, then I'm going to bed." She picks up the towel and walks out of the kitchen.

The kitchen slowly dissolves into air and a bedroom appears in its place. His mother lies in bed with a man but he can't see his face. The man whispers in her ear and holds her in his arms. Gerald frowns.

*This must be his father. Gerald leans over
the bed to hear what he says and to see
his face. His mother sighs deeply and he
can feel her warm breath on his cheek.
Then, Gerald blinks and the bedroom
disappears.*

*Suddenly, it's daytime and Gerald is
standing outside his mother's house
underneath a carport. The man quickly
puts two beige suitcases in the back seat
of a Ford Falcon. He closes the door and
turns to Gerald. He sees his father's face
for the first time. Gerald looks deeply into
his penetrating eyes and takes in his
image carefully. His father has thick dark
hair—he's a nice looking man. His father
stops moving, hand frozen into place on
the door handle, his body still like a
statue. And something happens. His
father's hand becomes gnarled, his hair
gradually turns gray and thins at the
temples, and his upright posture slumps
over slightly. He ages before Gerald's
eyes like dawn creeping into morning.
Gerald now looks into old eyes and a
wrinkled face. His father has on a soiled
green jacket, dirty blue pants and is
holding a green suitcase. Gerald jumps.
The old man is his father.*

The image fades away and Gerald now
stares at the sink in the clinic. He
touches his wet shirt and remembers he

dropped the foot tub a few moments earlier. He turns around quickly and looks at the old man. The old man looks pale.

Gerald says, "You are...my father."

The old man stutters. "I...I..."

Gerald repeats. "You are my father!"

There's a long silence until his father says, "I didn't know until now."

He stares hard at his father and knows instantly that this is the truth. Gerald quietly fingers his wet shirt. The old man watches him closely.

Gerald clears his throat. "Why did you leave us? My mother never even spoke your name because it was too painful."

His father says, "I don't remember."

"I knew that would be your answer. I'll find you later to arrange a time when we can talk privately, away from here."

His father nods. They stand looking at each other for a few more moments, then Gerald mops up the water on the floor. The doctor comes in, thanks Gerald for his help and goes over to the old man. Gerald walks out of the clinic in a daze as his father watches him leave in stunned silence.

Chapter 27
ROAD TRIP

Later, Gerald drops off a pair of new boots for his father, realizing it will take a while to get used to the old man being his father. Gerald quickly leaves the shelter telling Lee he isn't feeling well. He drives around midtown and Buckhead, not seeing the office buildings and stores while his cell phone rings incessantly. All he sees in his mind's eye is his father standing in the carport holding a green suitcase.

Hours later, as the evening sets in, Gerald finally heads home. He calls Valerie to come over and pick up some dinner for them on the way. A distraught Gerald greets Valerie at the door and she immediately senses something is very wrong, but all her coaxing him to talk as they eat dinner has no effect. Then, finally, a few hours later, Gerald hesitantly tells Valerie what happened.

Valerie is shocked. "I...I...don't know what to say."

Gerald sits down next to her on the couch. "I don't understand why I'm meeting him now after all these years, and why he left my mother."

"Now you can find out," Valerie says hopefully.

"But he can't remember a damn thing," Gerald retorts.

"Then tell him about your life," Valerie says. "Maybe it'll help him remember."

Gerald nods. "I hadn't thought of that."

"It's just amazing how all this has played out," Valerie says, shaking her head in disbelief.

Gerald says, "Yeah."

She asks, "What's his name?"

Gerald says, "I don't know, he doesn't know and the vision didn't show me."

Valerie raises her eyebrows. "Your mother never told you?"

"No. And her parents died before I was born. There was no one around to ask. I never pushed my mother about it when I got older because I knew it brought up bad memories."

"Are you sure the vision is true?" Valerie asks. "I mean, maybe he's not your father."

Gerald looks intensely at Valerie. "The one thing I know is that there's a reason I was drawn to Open Door. As soon as I laid eyes on him I felt a strong connection between us that couldn't be explained until now. I knew instantly once I saw the vision that he was my father."

Valerie is somewhat overwhelmed by the power of Gerald's words. And she's also scared of the old man—he's too powerful. She still cannot bring herself to do what he told her to do—tell Gerald the truth about her past.

Gerald breaks into her thoughts. "When I think about it, I came to volunteer at the shelter to make a change in my life. And I did. And now I meet him. But why? I don't know what kind of person he is. I thought he was a good guy because he turned in stolen stuff. But, my dad left us. How do I reconcile that?"

Valerie sighs. "I think you need to spend time with him, really get to know him and find out why he can't remember his own past."

Gerald looks thoughtful. "You're right. Maybe an overnight road trip with him—"

Valerie smiles. "That's a great idea."

Later, when Gerald and Valerie are in bed, he tosses and turns all night. He dreams about pieces of a previous dream in which the old man and the green suitcase are glowing, and standing in a room with a brown sofa and Oriental rug. Then he dreams of being in a large canyon asking questions to a distant figure standing on the other side: Who is my father? Who is the old man?

In the morning Gerald talks to his father at the shelter and invites him to drive to Jasper, Georgia the next day. At first Gerald's father says he doesn't want to go. He's not used to being around people, which makes being around his new-found son particularly challenging. He has no idea how to be a father. It's so much easier being a loner, especially if you didn't have a past. But, curiosity about who he really is overcomes Gerald's father. And his inner voice whispers that going with Gerald will give him answers. So, he changes his mind and decides to go on the trip after all.

Gerald picks him up at the shelter on shower day. He gets into the car and puts the green suitcase on the floor in front of him. Gerald remembers how protective he is of the suitcase. Gerald notices that the old man looks neater than usual.

Gerald drives off and his father bends down to tie his loose boot laces. "Thanks for the work boots, very sturdy. They should last for a long time."

"No problem. How are your feet doing?"

"Much better. The doc did his thing." He looks at Gerald sideways and adds, "And you having me soak them helped, too."

Gerald points to the backseat. "Good. By the way, I bought you some clothes for the trip."

He turns around and sees a shopping bag with a shirt and pants bulging from the top.

Gerald reaches into the back seat and pulls a soft drink out of a smaller bag and hands it to him. "In case you get thirsty."

His father nods as Gerald turns onto the 75-North expressway. "How far is Jasper?"

"About an hour from here. Technically it's too short to be a real road trip," Gerald says with a little laugh.

The old man scratches his ear. "And, it's good for us to go away?"

Gerald looks over at him. "We have to talk and I don't bite. There's no privacy at the shelter. And, I wasn't sure if you felt comfortable at my house. This will be neutral ground."

His father looks uneasy. "If you say so."

"Obviously, this is awkward for us both."

"Yes."

As Gerald drives he pulls an old picture out of his shirt pocket and hands it to his father. "What can you remember about my mom?"

His father looks at the photograph, at the smiling face with dimples flashing on both cheeks. Five-year-old Gerald sits on her lap. Gerald's father shrugs. "She's pretty. But like I told you before, I don't remember anything. Is she still alive?"

Gerald shakes his head. "No, she died six years ago. I was hoping that you would remember something about her."

A sad look comes over his father's face.

"I just wonder why you would ever leave my mom. She was a wonderful woman."

His father looks down at his lap. "I have no idea."

Gerald turns on the radio to fill up the awkward silence and they drive another twenty minutes without speaking. His father opens a can of Coke and gulps the drink noisily.

Once they hit 575-North, Gerald turns the radio off. "Tell me about yourself."

His father nervously shifts in his seat. "There's nothing much to tell."

"Sure there is. Do you have any friends? I think I've seen you talking to a guy at lunch sometimes."

His father scratches his head. "I mainly keep to myself, but I like Eddie, the one you've seen me with."

"What things do you like?"

His father ponders for a moment, then says, "Let me think...well, one time I had a pocket radio and would listen to the oldies station."

"I like music, too," Gerald says.

His father changes the subject. "I heard you run a big business. Surprised you have time to come to the shelter as much as you do."

Gerald smiles. "I find that coming to the shelter is much more fulfilling than some of the work I do. I like being around the residents."

He smiles slightly hearing Gerald's sincerity. He realizes that Gerald deserves to have a good father. Maybe he can try to be that for him.

For the first time since he learned he was Gerald's father, he doesn't feel as unsure and nervous. "You're a good person."

"Not always, but I'm changing working to be better."

Gerald's smile slowly fades away as he thinks about the times he and his mother volunteered at various church soup kitchens growing up.

He asks abruptly, "Are *you* a good person?"

His father is caught off guard. "I...don't know, I think I am."

"You don't know and I don't know you. All I know is that you left my mother and I want to know why."

He couldn't blame Gerald for feeling this way. "You should be angry. It was wrong of me to leave. I'm sorry."

"I just wish you could remember. Remember, damn it!" Gerald says harshly.

His father looks out the window at the highway signs. Gerald doesn't say anything for a long while, then finally, "I can't be mad and get to know you at the same time. My mom was a great mom. When she died several years ago I lost touch with things that really are important in life. She never remarried. It was just the two of us. Having a father around now would be—"

His father feels bad. "If I remember even the slightest bit, I will tell you."

Gerald stares hard at him.

His father shakes the empty soda can. "I need to pee...uhh...go to the bathroom, whenever you see a rest stop."

Gerald passes two more exits until he sees a sign that says: Pickens County Rest Area. They pull in.

He says, "We have about another 25 minutes until we get to Woodbridge Inn, where we're staying."

His father gets out, grabs the clothes Gerald bought and quickly goes to the bathroom carrying his green suitcase. Only a few cars are around.

His bladder is ready to burst as he steps up to the urinal to relieve himself. "Ahh, much better." The lights are low in the bathroom and Gerald's father squints at the mirror, looking at his wrinkled face. He runs water and splashes some on his face. His eyes are bloodshot. He's tired and knows that this will be a long, short trip. But, he will try his best to make this right for Gerald, his son. "*My* son. I have a son." Gerald's father stares in the mirror as if expecting his reflection to say something wise and soothing. He smirks, then bends down to put the new clothes into the green suitcase.

He pokes at the red and white fabric that hangs outside the suitcase before opening it. He throws the clothes inside and a gurgling sound like stew cooking on top of a stove comes from the bottom of the suitcase. Gerald's father curiously looks down and lifts clothes. The noise gets louder. Two voices are talking at the same time, their garbled voices tangle together, getting louder like a car radio coming into range. A male voice is talking and a female voice is crying and yelling. The air gets heavy in front of him and he feels thoughts invading his brain like a marching army. His wrinkles, temples and eyes pulsate with pounding, and pressure builds inside his head like a sinus cold. He squeezes his eyes shut.

A big gust of air pushes clothes in the air and a holey white t-shirt pops him on the face. He falls on his butt on the dingy, cold tile floor and yells "ouch" at the same time that a female voice yells "ouch."

He quickly opens his eyes and is suddenly standing up, looking down at Gerald's mother when she was young. She's on the linoleum floor, up on her elbows, in a dark kitchen.

She sniffles and rubs her eyes. "What is wrong with you?"

Something clicks in his mind, as if he's watching a stage play with familiar actors. He begins to remember—what is her name? It starts with a "J" he thinks.

He stands a foot away from the scene as a younger version of himself staggers over to her. "Jessica, I'm...."

He looks a mess, white shirt half pulled out of wrinkled black pants, hair a riot all over his head, and bloodshot eyes. He drops a half full bottle of whiskey on the floor and it breaks.

She whispers, "Shh. I just got Gerald to sleep."

"*You okay?*" *He asks.*

Gerald's father watches the scene unfold with dread gnawing at the pit of his stomach. He winces when she gets up slowly, smoothing down her blue nightgown.

Her right eye is puffy and half closed. "No, my eye, you hit me in my eye."

He reaches for Jessica and stumbles on the broken glass and says, "I won't do it againnn...I'm sor...ry." He's slurring so bad she can hardly understand what he's saying.

Gerald's mother begins to sob loudly and waves his hands away. "Don't touch me. Just get out!"

Gerald's father follows the drunk version of himself across the floor and steps back as he slides on shards of glass, trips over a chair and staggers out of the kitchen. He motions toward the door remembering what happens next as the scene unfolds: His drunk self passes out in the carport next to the Ford Falcon.

Gerald's father looks at the figure splayed on the ground with disgust. It seems he's watching himself for minutes but he knows that long ago when this actually happened, hours had passed when his younger self finally comes to and goes back inside the house.

He rubs his throbbing head as he slips quietly into the kitchen and goes to the bedroom. Jessica is asleep as he slides gently into bed next to her and cradles her in his arms. She stirs and opens her eyes.

He whispers, "Honey, I'm sorry. It won't happen again."

Jessica murmurs into his shoulder. "You always say that. You have to stop drinking."

"I know, and I will stop."

She says, "The last time you pushed me, the baby fell hard. If anything ever happened to him, I don't know what I would do." She lets out a deep sigh.

Gerald's father kisses Jessica on her forehead and whispers, "I love you. I love Gerald. I won't hurt you two again."

Jessica cries softly on his shoulder. He caresses and rocks her until she goes back to sleep. He kisses her hair and listens to her breathing for a long time, thinking about how out of control his drinking had gotten. Gerald's father knew the best thing for him to do was to leave before he seriously hurt them. He wasn't cut out to be a husband or a father and decides right then and there to pack up and leave the next day when a lady from church is coming to pick up Jessica and Gerald and go to an event at church. A *gust of air blows across the couple in bed and his head begins to pound.*

Then, the next moment Gerald's father is once again sitting on the cold tile in the bathroom staring at scattered clothes on the floor. He slowly gets up and leans against the sink because his legs are trembling. Gerald's father can't remember his name or anything else about his past. Riddled with shame, he can't bear to look at himself in the mirror. How could he be an abusive drunk? Once Gerald knows what happened he would surely hate him.

Chapter 28
STARTED THEN ENDED

Gerald's father snatches the clothes off the bathroom floor and quickly stuffs them inside the green suitcase. His heart gallops in his chest like horses running across a plain. Sweat slides down his face as he takes a peek outside. Gerald's in the car fiddling with his cell phone. This is a good time to make a run for it. There are woods behind the rest stop and he can hide out there for a day. He has to run. Wait a minute, what is he thinking? He can't run. He promised to tell Gerald if he remembered anything. Gerald's father looks at the woods. He can't run away like a wild animal. He turns back and sees Gerald is now leaning against the car, watching him. Deep inside he knows he has to do the right thing especially since he didn't do the right thing a long time ago. He takes a deep breath, wipes the sweat from his brow and walks to the car.

They drive to the hotel which is hidden down a long, winding road surrounded by woods. They check in and have dinner in the hotel's small dining room, Gerald is very talkative. Gerald's father doesn't want to talk at all and tells him that he's tired. Gerald knows he's a man of few words but senses something different about his mood tonight. Maybe he's nervous. Gerald makes some small talk while his father picks at his food.

After dinner, Gerald goes to bed and is happy that anger didn't cloud the day and get the best of him. He knows that patience and understanding aren't his strong suits. He's surprised to be handling this situation as well as he is and knows it's good for him to work on these things. Gerald actually looks forward to spending more time with his father.

In the next room, Gerald's father gets out of a warm bath and towels dry. It's nice to be able to take a bath instead of showering once a week at the shelter. He's also glad that he and Gerald have separate rooms so he can be alone and think. Gerald's father gets in the bed and adjusts the pillows over and over again, but can't seem to get comfortable. He looks toward the window and realizes what's wrong: he's not lying outside on the ground where the noises of the street and the night keep him company until sleep comes. He's not used to the quiet. He quickly dresses and goes outside where, in the chilly night air, he's finally able to think. Gerald's father thinks about how he met his son, the way he kept running into him, the way he kept giving Gerald visions. Is this God's way for him to deal with the past? He isn't really a religious man but there's no denying that everything happening is beyond his control. He certainly has no control of the truth. Once he tells his son the truth, there's no controlling Gerald's reaction, either. Gerald is a good man and he doesn't want to ruin his life. He shakes his head and mumbles, "Why does life have to be so damn complicated?" and goes back inside the hotel.

The next morning they eat a breakfast buffet at the hotel. Gerald's father is still quieter than normal. Gerald eyes the green suitcase sitting next to his father. "Why did you bring your suitcase? We're going back to the room before checking out."

"It goes where I go," Gerald's father says.

"No one is going to steal it."

His father repeats, "It goes where I go."

Gerald nods. "Whatever floats your boat." He tries to lighten the moment. "I guess it's like me taking a briefcase to the office."

His father is tackling a heaping plate of sausage, biscuits, gravy and grits.

Gerald is quiet and the old man can tell that Gerald expects him to say something in response. He gulps down some food. "What do you do when you're not at your office or working at Open Door?"

"I play tennis, collect wine, go to art galleries, and spend a lot of time with Valerie."

The old man wipes away some gravy that has spilled on his chin. "She seems nice."

Gerald smiles. "She's very nice. Which makes me wonder if the vision you gave me about marrying someone else is a mistake."

His father shrugs. "Just wait and see what happens."

Gerald says, "Okay, I'll let it go. I know you don't like discussing it."

Gerald's father changes the subject. "You certainly stay very busy."

"Well, my mother always stayed busy. We were always volunteering together when she wasn't at the pottery studio she owned. I still keep it open. Maybe I can take you by there one day."

Gerald's father nods. "Hmm."

The waitress comes by with a coffee refill for Gerald. "I was thinking that later this week we can get together again for dinner at my house."

His father nods again. "Hmm."

"I was also thinking that maybe you can stay with me after we get, uh, comfortable with each other," Gerald says. His father's eyes widen. "You can stay a few days a week if you don't want to stay every day. No pressure. I just figured you would like to get off the street. I'm sure you miss sleeping in a bed."

His father takes a big bite of a sausage link. "I miss a lot of things, like eating sausage and biscuits."

Gerald chuckles. "I can tell. I don't eat this way most of the time and sometimes miss it. I started exercising and I'm watching what I eat. I lost about fourteen pounds."

"Hmm."

Gerald sips some coffee. "You don't seem too enthused about my suggestion."

Gerald's father says quietly, "Thanks for the offer."

"Think about it and we'll discuss it next time we get together."

His father drops his fork down on the plate and says abruptly, "I remember why I left your mom."

Gerald looks surprised. "I wondered why you've been acting strange. What do you remember?"

He lowers his eyes. "I was a drunk."

Gerald takes a moment to think. "Why didn't she ever tell me?"

After a few moments of silence Gerald's father gulps down some apple juice and says reluctantly, "I hurt her...and you."

Gerald's mouth tightens. "What?"

His father finally looks up. "I hit her...I was abusive to both of you."

Gerald stares at him for a long time. He turns red and clenches his fists on top of the table. He motions to the waitress for the bill. Gerald pays the bill and leaves, almost knocking his chair to the floor. Gerald's father goes outside. Ten minutes later Gerald walks out with his small weekend bag, tosses it violently into the trunk, and gets in the car. His father gets in and Gerald drives away.

After driving in silence for several miles Gerald asks, "Is there anything else you remember?" His voice is tinged with anger.

"No. I'm sor—"

Gerald explodes. "I don't want to hear your damn I'm sorrys!"

"I wish it had never happened."

For a while Gerald drives at breakneck speed. His father nervously looks over at the speedometer—it reads 90. Gerald finally calms down and slows to 70 mph when they get into the Atlanta city limits.

He says coldly, "I knew that whatever it was you had done had to be horrible since my mother never remarried and never trusted men." Gerald's voice gets louder, his words flicking like a whip. "Actually, I'm glad you don't remember more because I'm sure you did many bad things. That's probably why you can't remember."

Gerald's father winces. "You're probably right."

"The one thing I want you to remember for the rest of your life is that I hate you and don't want to ever see you again!" Gerald spits the words out.

His father hangs his head in shame. He expected Gerald to react this way, but to actually hear the words is devastating. Gerald says no more. His face is like stone as he drives into Atlanta. The sky matches his mood, overcast with no sun in sight. They pull up to the shelter and Gerald's father gets out without a passing look from Gerald.

Gerald's father slowly walks toward the courtyard at the same time that Chantal walks from the office to the front door. She saw the old man get out of Gerald's car and wonders where they went. He doesn't see her looking through

the window. The old man's head hangs
down. She stares at him until he walks
away. Chantal isn't the only who's
watching. Even though it's too early in
the day for the courtyard to be filled with
people, someone looms near the other
side of the house, at the street corner.
Sinister, dark eyes attentively watch the
old man's moves. The old man walks
away from the shelter and down the
street as a car pulls up to the shelter and
three people walk past the house. A man
steps from the corner. He pulls a pack of
cigarettes from underneath his shirt
sleeve and there's a pineapple tattoo on
his forearm. He's pissed that too many
people are around for him to get to the
old man. He vows to keep trying for his
brother's sake and leaves.

The old man needs to get away from
Open Door. As he walks, every step he
takes feels heavy and burdensome. He
walks several blocks to the Kroger
grocery store on Ponce de Leon and goes
behind the store. He sits on top of his
suitcase. He puts his head into his hands
and sits that way for several moments.
An image flashes inside his head of him
looking angry. The old man raises his
head as the memory starts to unravel
like a knit sweater with a hanging piece
of string that you pull. He wrinkles his

brow in concentration to pull on that string. Bits and pieces of the past flash into his mind like photos being snapped quickly.

Snap. His hand swings in the air, he can see his flexed knuckles. Snap. Gerald's mother head pops to the right side, his fist hits her left cheek. Snap. She cries out as she falls down concrete steps. Snap. She grabs at her torn stockings. Snap. She rubs her chafed, bloody knees. Snap. He sees the side of a building and hears Gerald crying in the background but can't see him. Snap. He sees his wife's tear stained face up close, makeup running, smeared red lipstick. Her sobs echo deep in his head absorbing into all his senses. The sound slides away into silence then—Snap. He's on the floor with a man and they're brawling. The old man's fists are pounding the guy's face while the guy is pounding him on the chest and kicking him. The guy gasps out something that ends with, "…get the money."

The old man stands up and shakes his head, shakes away the memories. He vaguely remembers getting into a fight with this man, but not who he is and what the fight was about. He doesn't want to unravel anything else, he doesn't want to face who he really is. He believes he is a bad person just like Gerald said. He looks into the sky and cries for the son he has hurt. His tears are angry, bitter tears, tears of regret and shame. He drops to his knees, surprised by the intensity of his emotions. But learning more about his true self makes him sick to his stomach. For the first time in his life he feels truly alone. It's one thing to be alone by choice, but now he has to be alone because he isn't worthy of being around anyone or even having breath go through his body. He says aloud, "I wish I was dead."

Right after Gerald drops off his father, he calls Valerie at the boutique, then goes straight to her apartment. She meets Gerald there. As soon as she walks in the door, he blurts out what happened.

Valerie puts her purse and keys on the table and sits down on the couch in the living room. "Oh, God. I can't believe it."

"That makes two of us," Gerald says angrily.

She looks at his red, scowling face. "Where is he now?"

"I didn't leave him stranded there. Though I wanted to do that and so much more. I dropped him at Open Door."

"I don't know what to say."

Gerald sits down next to her. "There's nothing to say. I won't talk to him ever again."

Valerie shakes her head. "But he's at the shelter all the time."

Gerald throws his hands up. "I don't have to be there as much, though I'd hate to do that. Maybe he won't come around much since he knows how I feel."

"That will look strange to Lee. She'll ask questions."

"I'll come up with some excuse."

"And, more importantly you're not talking about this with your father."

Gerald explodes. "Don't call him that! And there's nothing to talk about. I don't want to talk to him."

She takes Gerald's hand. "Listen to me. A lot of good things have happened to you since being at Open Door. You've made a lot of good changes. Don't let this set you back."

"You're not going to get me to change my mind. I have every right to be mad."

Valerie thinks about her mother and says, "You should be mad, it's only natural. Sometimes those closest to us, hurt us the most. I think he's a different man now. Maybe you need to work on forgiving him."

Gerald snatches his hand away and jumps up. "I will never forgive him!" he screams loudly, then lowers his voice. "Sorry for yelling."

Valerie says quietly, "I understand. I'm just trying to help."

"I know, sweetheart. And I appreciate that. But, I don't think anything you say can help."

They hug each other. Gerald kisses her. She lays her head on his chest and he strokes her hair. "I know you care about me. You're special, unlike any other woman I've ever been with."

Valerie looks up at him. "You're special to me, too."

They stare at each other intensely for a few moments. Gerald gently traces the side of her face with his fingertips. Her skin is soft and her eyes are glowing.

"I love you, Val."

Her eyes get misty and she chokes up. "I love you."

Gerald kisses her again and they hold each other. "I will—we will get through this. It's over before it even started."

Valerie nods. She will talk to Gerald again later after he cools down. Maybe eventually he will talk to his father, she thinks, but not too hopefully.

Chapter 29
BACKSLIDING & SLIDING BACK

Two months go by and Gerald hardly goes to the shelter, except to drop off checks at the beginning of each month and some kitchen and cleaning supplies. Lately, sixty-hour work weeks have replaced his volunteering. Closing new big deals has shut him off from everyone. But if anyone can get through to Gerald it would be Valerie.

Today is one of those days where she tries yet again to pull him out of the quicksand of his old ways. Valerie goes to Gerald's office to find Karen hunkered over a tall pile of folders on her desk. It's getting late and Valerie can see how tired she looks.

"Karen, go home and I'll finish up here," Valerie says.

Karen shakes her head. "No, Gerald wants me to finish this—"

"Don't worry about Gerald. I know how to handle him," Valerie insists.

Karen smiles and grabs her purse. "Thanks! You're a sweetheart." Karen leaves as Valerie goes to Gerald's office door. She knocks and opens the door. Gerald is sitting in a leather chair. Various pictures of him with the Atlanta mayor and local businessmen are on the wall behind him. Gerald is just getting off a phone call.

Valerie pecks Gerald on the cheek. "Hi, baby. I sent Karen home. She was exhausted."

At first Gerald looks irritated, then Valerie gives him a knowing look. "Okay, I'm not mad. She needed a break."

"Good, be nice and stop being a slave driver."

He turns to check something on his laptop. "You're right, you're right."

"Why don't you leave early, too? We could catch a movie up the street."

"I can't. I'm slammed with work."

Valerie sits down. "Gerald, you have to stop pushing yourself like this. Remember how you used to be spontaneous and have fun?"

Gerald looks up from the computer. "Val, I have a business to run."

"I know, but you didn't work like this before your fight with—"

Gerald interrupts and looks sharply at Valerie. "Not again Val, I'm tired of this discussion."

"I keep bringing it up because you've changed so completely after meeting your father. You just can't be mad at him forever."

Gerald yells, "Oh, yes I can!"

"Gerald, you're angry and taking it out on everyone around you," Valerie says, her voice firm. "We hardly go out anymore, you work too much, your poor assistant is working too much, you even stopped volunteering at Open Door. You stopped doing the things you enjoy. Stop this. You're only hurting yourself."

Gerald stares angrily at Valerie. She says quietly, "I'm only telling you this because I love you and hate to see you in pain. At least think about. I'm taking Karen's work with me and I'll do it at home." Valerie leaves.

Gerald sits at his desk staring blindly at the computer. Val is right. He sighs deeply. He's making life miserable for her, his friends, and business associates. And he misses being at the shelter. He shuts off his computer, but still sits at the desk engulfed in sadness.

* * *

It has been raining steadily for a few days, turning all of Atlanta into a grim, grey canvas. The wet chill has seeped into every pore of the tired old man as he stands near the bus stop close to the Carter Center. Since the encounter with his son a couple of months ago he has been deeply depressed. He keeps replaying in his mind what he did to Gerald's mother. The old man hasn't been to the shelter for fear of running into Gerald. He can't bear to see the hate in his eyes. And he hasn't been to any other shelter or soup kitchen in town. Instead, he forages for food in garbage cans behind restaurants and occasionally begs for money. The old man doesn't want to eat but absentmindedly forces what scraps he comes across down his throat. He looks at the spot where he usually sleeps and wishes that there was a continual night so he could be alone, away from people, to lie down forever in the grass in front of the bus stop. Right now though, he just stares sadly into the drizzle.

A horn honks and a white van drives by slowly. It circles the block, then honks again. The old man isn't paying attention.

Then a voice yells, "Are you okay!?"

The van stops on the side of the street, right in front of him. The driver's side window rolls down. He's surprised to see Lee leaning over the seat looking at him.

He yells back, "I'm fine." But his words only come out as squeaks.

Lee looks worried and opens the door. "Get in, you look sick. You need to get out of this weather." The old man looks away. Lee says, "Please get in. I'm not leaving until you do."

By this time cars are slowing down to see what's going on. The old man doesn't want attention. He slowly walks to the van and gets in. Lee is frightened at his appearance. He has lost too much weight. His face is gaunt and his eyes are sunk in a bit.

She quickly closes the window and turns up the heat. "I haven't seen you in awhile. I'm glad I was driving by. Let's get back home so you can eat something."

The old man rubs his arms to warm them up. "Thanks, Miss Lee."

"You had me so worried. I'm glad I found you."

As soon as they arrive at the shelter and go inside, the old man glances over his shoulder as if looking for someone. "I won't stay long."

"You don't have to rush off," Lee says. "At least stay long enough to shower, change clothes, and eat."

They head upstairs as Chantal is coming down. The old man keeps looking over his shoulder again, then goes into the bathroom.

Chantal follows her mother into the kitchen as Lee takes out some bread and ham from the refrigerator.

She asks Lee, "What's going on? He hasn't been here in a long time."

Lee puts on a hairnet and some gloves and starts to make a sandwich. "I just happened to drive by the Carter Center and saw him."

"He looks awful," Chantal says.

Lee nods. "Yes, he does. He hasn't been eating much."

Lee puts two slices of bread on a plate and spreads a bit of mayonnaise on them, then adds some lettuce. "Please get something for him to drink."

Chantal opens the refrigerator and takes out a pitcher of iced tea. "I wonder where he's been all this time."

Lee finishes making the sandwich. "I have no idea, but I'm glad he's here now. I'm sure he'll never tell us where he's been."

Gerald comes into the kitchen with boxes of plastic forks and paper plates. "We just got this donation from an office near Inman Park; should last for a couple of months."

"Great, we really needed these," Lee says.

Gerald looks at the sandwich on the counter. "You should have called me. I would have brought you something."

"It's not for me," Lee says. "It's for the man with the green suitcase. I just picked him up."

Gerald's eyes widen with surprise. He stops unpacking the boxes and gets very still. "He's here?"

"Yes, he is," Lee replies. "He's upstairs taking a shower. Let me go see if he's ready to eat."

A strange look comes across Gerald's face. "No...no...I'll go tell him—" He abruptly walks out of the kitchen.

Chantal and Lee look at each other and Chantal says, "I wonder what's going on. They've both been away from the shelter for awhile. This happened right after I saw Gerald drop off the old man that day. Remember, I told you how upset the old man was? Gerald came back last week and now the old man comes back today."

Lee's eyes flicker with recognition. She automatically knows that whatever is going on probably has to do with the old man showing a vision to Gerald.

"It's probably just coincidence. Don't give it too much thought," Lee says to her daughter.

"Mom," Chantal says, "You're a lousy liar." Lee gives Chantal a playful poke in the ribs.

Gerald is upstairs, and stands outside the door of the men's shower area and leans against the wall. Gerald hears the shower running. The old man coughs loudly, then after a few minutes, the water stops. The old man dries off and gets dressed in the clean clothes Lee gave him. Gerald waits for his father to come out.

When he does, he immediately sees Gerald. "Wha—?"

They stare at each other in shock. Gerald can't believe how skinny his father has become.

After a few more moments, Gerald finally finds his voice. "Lee has the food ready downstairs."

"Okay," his father mumbles.

"You don't look good. Are you okay?" Gerald asks.

The old man looks down. "I'm okay."

"You don't look it. You need to eat and get some rest."

"Why?" His father asks.

"What do you mean, *why*? Because you need to take care of yourself."

The old man coughs, his chest rattling. "Why do you care?"

That sound pricks at Gerald's emotions. "I...I...guess I don't want anything to happen to you."

The old man is surprised, echoing what Gerald feels. "Oh."

"I didn't think you would ever come back here. Hell, I didn't think I would ever come back here. But, I'm glad we're both here now. I'm still mad, but I just realized that I don't hate you so much that I want something bad to happen to you."

His father is quiet for several minutes and then says, "I appreciate that."

"I know what happened in the past but I have to live and deal with what's happening now," Gerald says. "I have to consider that you may be different now from that horrible person you once was."

"I am different," The old man says.

Gerald looks deeply into his eyes. "Even if you aren't, I have to...to forgive you, if I'm to have any peace for myself." Gerald takes a deep breath. "Forgive me for not forgiving you. That wasn't right to not forgive you from before, but I'm working on forgiving you now."

The old man is overcome. He never thought he would see his son again, let alone hear these words. "Forgive me for hurting your mother and you."

As they stand there looking at each other, Gerald hears the words he just said to his father: "Forgive me for not forgiving you." They seem familiar, like something from a dream. Yes, he remembers—he said these words in a dream months ago, right before he found out the old man was his father.

Gerald's eyes light up. "This is supposed to happen."

The old man tilts his head. "Hmm?"

"I dreamed about this, about asking you to forgive me for not forgiving you."

His father smiles a little. "Is that so?"

Gerald smiles back. "You appeared at the very end of my dream. I think you were in the dream the whole time, but I couldn't see you until the end. I had no idea why I was saying those words and why you were in the dream, until now."

"I guess things happen for a reason."

Gerald nods. "Yes, they do. Which is why I have to work on what's happening to us now."

Gerald extends his hand to his father who now wonders if it's possible that he can have a relationship with his son.

Chapter 30
SEEING…BEAUTY

Hope can heal and it can bring about great change. Hope is what clings to the old man as he finally takes Gerald's hand into his and squeezes tightly. His other hand holds the green suitcase. The red and white fabrics sticking out of it begin to glow with a moving light like a swarm of fireflies. Gerald remembers his father holding the green suitcase and glowing in a dream he had months ago. The old man looks peaceful and his face begins to glow, the wrinkles on his face begin to vibrate. Gerald feels his hand getting very warm and sees his father's hand is glowing red with heat. He doesn't pull away though. A wave of heat slides up his body.

A voice trickles into Gerald's mind. "Close your eyes." It's his father's voice inside his head though he is standing right in front of Gerald and his lips aren't moving.

Gerald closes his eyes. He feels the old man's spirit enter his body, like the hint of a passing thought coming back into the mind. And then images flash into his head; they're quick but vivid. He sees himself smiling, standing next to Valerie. They're holding hands and she is smiling, too. The scene quickly fades to the old man lying on the floor with a peaceful smile on his face. Very peaceful. Gerald feels deeply connected to them both. The strong sense of togetherness overcomes him. Then his mind becomes a blank sheet of paper, darkness fills the space where the images were a few moments ago. His body is still hot.

Gerald opens his eyes and sees his father's face still glowing and vibrating. "I guess everything works out for us all."

The old man nods and says softly, "Things always work out the way they were meant to be."

Gerald points to the fabrics sticking out of the green suitcase—they are still glowing. "Is the glowing normal?"

The old man hesitates. "No, I was…surprised."

Gerald senses there's something more his father isn't saying. "I know you're very protective of your suitcase. It's never out of your sight."

"All I own is in there," the old man says.

Gerald bookmarks his suspicion for a later time. He sees the peaceful look on his father's face and thinks he looked even more peaceful in the vision he just had.

Meanwhile downstairs, Chantal and Lee have finished unpacking the plates and utensils that Gerald brought in earlier and are now in the office working on donation receipts. Chantal tells her mother she's going home. Chantal calls a taxi, then realizes she left her favorite ring in the upstairs bathroom.

She hurries upstairs. Around the corner she hears Gerald talking to the old man. The air feels hot as a sauna as she gets closer. She wipes sweat from her brow as she peeks around the corner. Chantal sees the old man's face glowing and his wrinkles vibrating. Gerald and the old man are holding hands. And she sees both their hands glowing and the red and white fabrics hanging out of the suitcase are glowing, too. Chantal blinks several times to make sure what she's seeing is real.

The old man slowly takes his hand from Gerald's hand. His face gradually loses its brightness and the wrinkles slow their movements. The fabrics lose their brightness, too.

"Everything is okay," the old man says.

Gerald hugs him. "I know it is...father. You've healed me. Your power is great."

Gerald's father looks surprised and hugs him back. Then he shakes his head. "I have no power."

Gerald smiles. "The fact that you say you don't means that you do. Thank you."

Chantal almost gasps out loud when she hears this. She silently walks back down the stairs in shock. Chantal stands in the foyer, shaking, her mind racing. She quickly leaves. Chantal can't believe that the old man is Gerald's father and doesn't understand why this is a secret. Then her mind focuses on something Gerald said: his father had strong healing powers. Chantal smiles. She remembers how the old man glowed, as well as the fabrics hanging out of the old green suitcase. Chantal knows that he can heal her. Oh, to be beautiful again! She could go back to her life of living in France and singing again. Maybe David would even be with her again. And if he didn't, she would always find someone else. Chantal wonders when she can get the old man alone so she can ask him to heal her.

Upstairs, Gerald is talking to his father. "I just thought about something. I still don't know your name. Do you remember it?"

Gerald's father shakes his head. "I would like to know, too."

"Maybe you will remember it soon."

"Maybe." His father didn't sound convinced.

"In the meantime, I would like you to come stay with me so we can spend more time together."

His father looks surprised. "Oh."

"You will have lots of space and I'll cook for us."

Gerald's father hesitates. "I don't know."

"Well, I don't want you on the street."

"That's nice of you, but I can't." He looks down at the suitcase.

Gerald scratches his head. "Why don't you want to stay with me?"

Gerald's father thinks about the suitcase and knows he can't ever let anyone find out about it. This was more important than disappointing his son again. Being by himself, he didn't have to deal with anyone asking questions about it. Gerald had already asked about the suitcase and he would do so again.

"I'm so used to being on the street. I don't know if I can live with anyone."

"I tell you what, I won't pressure you," Gerald says. "We'll take it slow. I'll get you an apartment near Open Door until you feel comfortable staying with me."

Gerald's father looks worried. "Don't spend any money."

Gerald smiles. "I want to. I want to take care of you. Anyway, I know the landlord of the building where you'll live so it won't cost anything."

Gerald's father looks relieved. "Good."

Gerald's eyes twinkle mischievously. "Yes, it is good. I'm the landlord, I own the building." Gerald chuckles.

Gerald's father grunts. "Well then."

He's obviously relieved that he doesn't have to live with his son. He must guard the green suitcase carefully. It's important that its secret stay with him.

Chapter 31
NEW THINGS

As Gerald gets the apartment ready for his father to move in, it reminds him of the time he bought his mother a house and she went shopping with him for some new furniture. His father, on the other hand, refused to even look at a catalog to pick out some pieces of furniture and just grumbled that if Gerald kept asking, he was going to change his mind about moving into the apartment. Gerald finally gets the old man to say that brown is his favorite color and he didn't want anything fancy.

When Gerald takes his father to the apartment, his eyes rove around the room and immediately spot the dark brown couch in the living room.

He walks over to it and rubs the thick suede fabric. "I like this."

"Good." Gerald walks to the window. "Dad, get comfortable. Sit down, this is *your* place."

He sits down stiffly, like he's waiting in a doctor's office. Gerald's father stares down at the brown and white Oriental rug on the floor in front of him. "This rug looks pretty expensive."

"Don't worry. I didn't buy it. The last tenant left it along with some other things."

Gerald's father nods. "Thanks for everything."

Gerald adjusts the brown curtains at the window. "You know, dad, I dreamed about you being here at the apartment."

"Unh-huh," his father says, slightly surprised.

"I saw this exact sofa and rug."

"Did you now? That's interesting."

"Yes, it is. You were in my dream, and so was my ex-business partner. He was telling me about going bankrupt. I thought he meant that I was going to be bankrupt. But then he dropped the lawsuit because *he* was going bankrupt in real life. Do you remember the dream?"

Gerald's father shakes his head. "I could feel that I was in your bedroom. My energy was going to you."

Gerald looks thoughtfully. "I felt that energy. I've had two dreams like this. I think some of your power temporarily passes on to me. Have you been able to do this before?"

"No. It's not something I do, it just happens. I think it happens to you because you're my son."

Gerald nods. "I think you're right. That makes sense." Gerald pauses. "Well, how about we go shopping? You need some new clothes."

His father murmurs, "I guess so."

As they leave Gerald's father grabs the green suitcase. "Dad, you don't need that old thing. I'll get you a new suitcase. Throw that one out."

His father flinches as if someone hit him. "No, I won't throw this out! I like my suitcase." He tightly grasps it to his chest.

"I'm sorry. Didn't mean to upset you. I just thought you would want a new one."

Gerald's father calms down and shakes his head. "I don't want a new one."

Gerald pats him on the back. "Whatever you want to do is fine. C'mon, let's go."

As they walk out of the apartment Gerald looks at the green suitcase with its white and red fabrics hanging out, and wonders why his father is so attached to it. The suspicion Gerald bookmarked the other day comes to mind: his father's evasiveness about the glowing fabrics when he was giving the vision to Gerald at the shelter.

Later, after going to Macy's and buying some new cargo pants, several shirts, a sweater and a few pairs of underwear, his father is exhausted and tells Gerald he needs to lie down and take a nap. Alone, he plops down on the cushy bed but finds it hard to sleep. He closes his eyes but just as he starts dozing, he's half dreaming, half remembering things from the past. He's fighting the same man he remembered back when Gerald dropped him at shelter after the road trip.

They're fighting. The man grunts as he falls down on top of a coffee table and it breaks in two. The man's eye is puffed up and red and his knuckles are bleeding. Gerald's father stumbles on top of him. They're both drunk. His lip is busted, blood trickling down his shirt and his nose is broken. The man moves from the broken table to the bare floor and mutters something that ends with "...get the money."

Gerald's father's eyes pop open and he sits up in bed. He's certain that this man was his friend and drinking buddy. He gambled a lot and always owed money. Damn, he probably owed a lot of money to this friend. He lies back down to drift off to sleep, hoping there will be no more memories.

Gerald's drive home is filled with thoughts about all the things that have come true from the visions. Only one vision isn't true—the one where his father shows him marrying his ex-girlfriend Christy. Gerald is certain that can never happen. But he's grateful that his father has come back into his life. "It was meant to be," he says aloud to himself as he pulls into the garage of his house.

Chapter 32
CAN'T HELP

Over the next several weeks Chantal grows more and more frustrated because she doesn't see the old man at the shelter. She can't ask Gerald or her mom without raising questions. She notices that Gerald isn't coming around as much and assumes he must be spending time with his father away from Open Door. Chantal is desperate to find a way to restore her lost beauty. She dreams of being able to look at her face in a mirror—her once beautiful face. Then she and David would walk on the beach in Nice with the wind blowing through her hair, and he'd be laughing at something funny she said. Chantal cannot bear to wake every morning knowing she's still disfigured—it has made her angry and deeply depressed.

* * *

One day, Gerald's father asks to be dropped off at Open Door while Gerald goes off to a business meeting. The old man misses being at the shelter even though he's a loner. He's even surprised he feels this way.

He smiles as he steps into the courtyard. He immediately spots Eddie standing near the water spout in front of the house.

"Hey, where have you been?" Eddie asks, coming over to the old man.

Gerald's father scratches his head. "I've been around. How've you been?"

Eddie eyeballs him and like a bloodhound, sniffs out that something is different about the old man, even though the old man had made sure to put on some of his old clothes and his usual threadbare green jacket, white shirt, and dark pants. The old man shifts uncomfortably from foot to foot, sensing that Eddie can tell something is different.

"I'm good," Eddie replies. "Getting ready to move into a small studio apartment since I've got a regular job now."

"What kind of job?"

Eddie notices something—he can't put his finger on it, then it clicks—how clean the old man looks. His hair is clean. And neatly trimmed. His face is clean. Even his nails are clean.

Eddie picks at the dirt under his nails. "I'm doing maintenance at the apartment complex I'm moving into." He grins. "My luck has finally changed."

The old man smiles. "I'm glad things are good now."

Chantal looks out the front door to see how many people are there before her mother comes out with the sign-up sheet for lunch. Chantal is so happy when she sees the old man talking to a homeless man she sees often. She didn't even know he had friends. Chantal senses that this is her chance to talk to him. She wants to make sure he's staying to eat so she can get him alone afterwards.

Chantal isn't the only one waiting for the old man to be alone. Just like he did awhile ago, the tall, big man with the long scruffy beard is walking down the street when he spots the old man talking to Eddie in the courtyard. He's smoking a cigarette and angrily flicks ashes out of his beard. He wants vengeance for his brother's incarceration.

When Lee shows up with the sign-in sheet, Chantal casually says, "The old man with the green suitcase is here. He looks much better than the last time you saw him."

Lee smiles. "Let me go talk to him."

Chantal follows her mother a little way into the courtyard, but then hangs back a few feet to hear what Lee says to the old man. When she sees that he's staying for lunch, Chantal can barely contain her excitement.

The lunch of sandwiches and potato salad is finally over. Chantal hovers near the front door, waiting anxiously. The tall man waits in the alley of a building next to Open Door, tugging on his beard and puffing on a cigarette. He steps out every few minutes to see when the old man leaves the courtyard.

Finally the old man leaves Open Door and walks down the street. The tall man tosses his cigarette, flicks a Swiss army knife from his pocket and walks toward him. The tall man curses loudly when he sees Chantal move quickly behind the old man. He ducks back into the alley.

Chantal catches up with the old man. "Hi, how are you?"

The old man stops, turns around and is surprised to see Chantal standing there.

"I'm fine," he says.

Chantal adjusts her sunglasses and looks at him critically. "You know I'm Lee's daughter," she says. "I just wanted to properly introduce myself."

The old man frowns slightly and wonders why she's talking to him. Eddie once told him that Chantal didn't like being around homeless people. "Okay." He turns back around and starts to walk away.

She smiles. "Wait a minute. Please." The old man stops and looks at her curiously. "I have a bit of a favor to ask you," she says. He senses she's a phony and wants to get away from her.

"You don't know this," Chantal continues, "but I was in a terrible accident and my face was badly burned. That's why I wear a scarf and sunglasses all the time. I was once a singer and a model, but this has killed my career. I need—"

He cuts in. "Listen, not to be rude, but I can't help you."

"I know you can help me," Chantal pleads. "I saw you heal Gerald. Can you please...please heal my face?"

The old man turns pale. All phoniness is gone, she sounds so pathetic now. "I didn't heal him. I don't *heal* people. And what are you doing snooping around anyway?"

"I won't tell anyone your secret," Chantal says. "I wasn't snooping. I went upstairs a few days ago. That's when I saw your power."

The old man realizes she now knows that Gerald is his son. He hates that she knows everything. "What you saw was something else," he says adamantly.

"Listen, if you want money, I'm willing to pay you," she pleads.

"It's not about money," he says. "I can't heal you."

"Please, I need my life back," Chantal cries. "Please help me."

"I can't help."

Chantal suddenly snatches off her large dark sunglasses and scarf. "Look at me, I'm a monster. I can't look like this anymore."

He looks in shock at the scarred and angry looking skin on the left side of her face. The other side of her face is smooth and clear. He suddenly wishes he could heal her.

He slowly shakes his head and walks away. The tall man peeks out from the alley and sees the old man walking away from Chantal.

He waits until the old man passes the alley where he's hiding, then follows him. Two police cars come up the street and the tall man quickly ducks back into the alley. The cops are still looking for him and he has to be careful—he can't get thrown in jail like his brother. The tall man waits until they pass to follow the old man again.

Chantal stands alone for a few moments as tears slide down her cheek. Chantal angrily wipes away her tears and puts her scarf and sunglasses back on. She won't give up; she'll figure out how to convince the old man to help her. "I have to," she mutters to herself. "I can't live this way anymore."

Chapter 33
DINNER

Valerie loves the new Gerald. He's happier, more relaxed, not working so hard, spending more time at Open Door, and spending more time with her. His smile, his walk, everything is radiating with happiness and everyone around him notices it. But when Gerald talks about his father, Valerie is haunted by the vision his father gave her, and about telling Gerald her secret. She just can't bring herself to do it.

Gerald is bringing his father home for dinner tonight and Valerie is cooking. She thinks about not having seen his father since he gave her the vision months ago. Lost in her thoughts she cuts her finger as she chops up some carrots and celery. She looks at her hand and notices it's shaking. Valerie drinks a glass of wine to calm her nerves.

Gerald gets to his father's apartment to find him wearing a white button down shirt and a brown tie with khaki slacks. "Dad, you didn't have to get dressed up," Gerald says.

Gerald's father pats his tie. "I thought it would be nice to do."

Gerald grins. "You know what, after dinner I'll have Val take some photos of us together."

Gerald's father says, "Okay." He pauses. "Gerald, someone was in my apartment yesterday when I was out, but nothing was taken. I didn't call the police—I hate dealing with them. But I may have to if this happens again."

"You should have called me," Gerald says. "That was the maintenance man. Since I moved you in so quickly some minor things needed repairing."

His father grumbles. "He sure left a mess."

Gerald frowns. "I don't like that. What did he do?"

Gerald's father quickly says, "It's no big deal. I just happen to notice everything since I'm not used to living in a place."

He doesn't want to get the maintenance man fired, and he doesn't mention that the refrigerator door was wide open (he could see smudged fingerprints on the silver door), or, that there was dirt tracked in on the living room floor when he came back home.

"Good, as long as everything is fine with you," Gerald says.

As they leave, Gerald's father drops his keys as he locks the door and notices some long, dark scraggly hairs near the doorway on the floor. He assumes the maintenance man should probably get a haircut.

Back at Gerald's house Valerie brings out baked chicken with roasted carrots, potatoes, and onions, and a spinach and tomato salad, while Gerald whips up some warm bacon dressing.

They sit at the dining room table and both Gerald and Valerie smile as they watch the old man eat with gusto, immediately digging into one of the three pieces of chicken piled on his plate. "This is very good, Valerie. Chicken is my favorite."

Gerald pours some water in Valerie's glass. "Why aren't you drinking wine?" his father says. "I know you love wine."

Gerald looks surprised, "I didn't want to—"

His father cuts in. "I don't drink, even before I met you, though I did way back in the past. You won't send me off the wagon."

Gerald smiles. "Just making sure."

Gerald gets some wine and glasses. He serves Valerie before pouring some for himself.

"Drinking caused so many problems for me in the past," Gerald's father says sadly.

Gerald sips some wine. "Well, let's not dwell on the past, dad. Let's just be here in the now."

Valerie nods in agreement, quietly sipping her wine and looking at Gerald's father, then she quickly looks away.

At the end of the evening and right before Gerald takes his father home, Valerie takes pictures of Gerald and his father with Gerald's cell phone. Then his father takes some of her and Gerald, both of them making silly, funny faces. After Gerald takes his father back to the apartment, the two men hug each other at the front door, both with tears in their eyes.

When Gerald gets back home, Valerie is already in bed watching an old Bette Davis movie. He kisses her and thanks her for the delicious dinner. "Now that my dad is settled I'll have him come over here more often. Then, hopefully, he can move in."

"That sounds great," Valerie says.

Gerald gets into bed. "I'm glad to have him around." Gerald leans over and kisses Valerie on the lips. "I'm happy that you're around, too."

Valerie puts her arms around his neck and kisses him back. "I'm glad to be around."

"You're not like any man I've known. You're kind, generous, forgiving, and you really like helping people."

They stare at each other as if seeing each other for the first time, then kiss passionately. Gerald lifts his head and says, "I love you Valerie."

"I love you too," Valerie replies breathlessly.

Valerie holds him tightly and they rock together gently. She feels shy as Gerald touches her, as though exploring her body is something new. When they make love they become lost in each other's energy and emotions.

Later, they talk quietly and cuddle in the midst of tangled sheets. Valerie has her head on Gerald's chest. He strokes her hair as he says, "I'm glad you didn't have a boyfriend when we met."

"I agree. And, I'm surprised you weren't married."

"I did have some long relationships, but just because a relationship is long doesn't necessarily mean it's serious. What about you, how long did your last serious relationship last?"

Valerie hesitates. "I've never had a serious relationship until now."

"Really? Why not?"

Valerie shrugs and rubs his chest. "Either it wasn't the right guy or the timing was off. Plus, a lot of times I was dealing with my mom."

"You've never really told me about your mother. I wish you would," Gerald says gently.

Valerie sighs. "Okay, here goes." Valerie hesitates again.

"Please, I want you to share things with me," Gerald says.

Valerie nods and begins in a shaky voice. "My mom is mentally ill. She has been as long as I can remember. It was hard growing up. When my dad died I had to take care of her. And sometimes she would disappear for weeks at a time. She doesn't stay on her meds which is why I don't see her much. It's hard to keep up with where she lives."

"Val, I'm sorry you have to go through this. I wish you had told me sooner."

Valerie's eyes are filled with tears. "It's a lot to deal with. The reason I came to volunteer at Open Door is because when I was in high school my mother had one of her episodes. She was missing and ended up there. So when you think about, my mom is responsible for me coming back to the shelter and meeting you."

Gerald smiles. "Well, that's a good way to look at it. I'd like to meet her one day."

"You would?

"Of course, she's a part of you. You don't have to be ashamed."

"Thanks, baby."

"I mean it, I'll always be there for you no matter what."

Valerie sits up, gathering the sheets around her chest and turns to look at him. "There's something else I need to tell you."

Gerald stares at Valerie. "Go ahead. Tell me, I want to hear."

Valerie looks away from Gerald and talks slowly. "Umm...well, it started when I was just out of high school and dealing with my mom. I needed money. I...was...I was...this is so hard to say...I was a paid escort." Valerie pauses to see the shocked look on Gerald's face. "I came to the shelter to volunteer right after I quit the business. I wanted to make a new start. I got the job at the boutique—the first time I had a regular job in years." She pauses and looks directly at Gerald. "When I saw your ex-business partner on T.V., the reason why I was so upset was because I knew him. He...he...was my former client." Valerie pauses to let the news sink in. "But you've changed how I feel about men. I had never liked men and had never had a real relationship until now. It's the past and all behind me now."

Gerald stares at Valerie with a blank look and is silent for what seems like an eternity. He sits beside her on the bed, but he's not there.

Finally, he says softly, "Get out."

She says, "Can we talk about—"

"Get out of my bed!" Gerald yells so loud that Valerie jumps. "Get out!"

Valerie cries as Gerald jumps out of the bed. "Please, Gerald."

He quickly goes to the closet, snatches her clothes off the hangers and throws them at her. She gets off the bed and holds the sheet around her.

Gerald says, "Don't say another word, just put your clothes on and get out. I don't want to ever see you again, you...you whore!" He spits the words out in disgust.

Gerald storms out of the bedroom. Valerie gets dressed quickly and has a hard time seeing her clothes through the tears streaming down her face. She puts her shirt on backwards and throws on jeans, balling the rest of her clothes, including her coat, in her hand. She walks on trembling legs to the garage. Gerald is nowhere in sight. She backs out of the driveway almost hitting his brick mailbox and drives two blocks away and into the parking lot of a drugstore. Valerie collapses across the passenger seat and breaks down, crying a river of tears.

Chapter 34
THE AFTERMATH

Chantal

Chantal and Lee are in the office at Open Door, working on a newsletter to post on the shelter's Web site. Chantal sneezes loudly.

"Bless you." Lee looks at her daughter. "You've been sniffling and coughing for the last two days. Go to my house and get into bed. Please don't go to the motel."

Chantal dabs her red nose with a tissue. For once she wants to go home. "You're right. I feel awful."

Chantal leaves as Lee says, "I'll be home as soon as I can."

Lee is worried about Chantal. She's been sick for a week with a cold and the previous week it was headaches.

Chantal walks slowly into her mother's house and pauses in the foyer. She looks at a picture of herself when she was ten years old. She has on a crown and a trophy is in her hand. It was taken when she had won first place in the Miss Young Atlanta beauty contest. She frowns at the picture, jealous of her own smiling face framed by long golden hair. She throws her purse at it, knocking it off the wall and breaking the glass. Chantal cries and collapses on the floor, depression overwhelming her. She hasn't been able to find the old man. Her sense of helplessness has become unbearable.

Gerald

Gerald goes back into his bedroom after Valerie leaves. The sight of the crumpled sheets on the floor and the scent of their lovemaking wafts in the air. Every emotion inside Gerald comes boiling to a head, screaming deep in his brain. She *was* a prostitute! Gerald wonders if she was even capable of loving him or anyone.

He has no one to talk to. He's too embarrassed to tell any of his close friends. What would he say? "Guess what, the woman I was in love with was a prostitute and slept with my ex-business partner." Gerald wonders if Valerie was sleeping with Tony when they started dating. It's ironic, he realizes, but if he had showed up when Tony invited him, and if Valerie had been available, he would have been a "client." And they never would have had a relationship and he wouldn't have fallen in love with her. Funny how the smallest change of an event can alter fate considerably.

He is numb. Hurt and disappointed, Gerald calls Karen and tells her he's taking a few days off from work. Three days go by and then Gerald tells Karen that he'll be working from home for a few weeks.

Gerald goes to the shelter one day and Lee tells him, "Valerie called a few days ago saying she was sick. Is she okay?"

"She's still feeling out of sorts," Gerald says abruptly.

Lee looks at Gerald closely. Circles are under his eyes and he looks tired. "You look sick, too. Something must be going around. Chantal has also been sick for a few weeks."

Gerald says, "I'll be okay."

Lee pats him on the arm. "Go home and get some rest. And tell Valerie I hope she feels better, too."

"Will do."

For Gerald, it's hard to get away from thinking about Valerie, especially when his father asks for copies of the pictures they took at dinner the night that Valerie cooked. Gerald pulls the pictures out of his nightstand drawer and flips through them. In one photo, Valerie is bent over laughing as Gerald tickles her. In another, he's kissing her on the cheek and she's grinning from ear to ear. Suddenly, they're too painful to look at. Gerald won't tell his father yet.

Gerald didn't have to tell his father anything. The old man knew when they got into the car, heading off to dinner, and Gerald stiffly hands the pictures to him. He sees the pain of Valerie's truth etched on his son's face. He knows that Valerie has told Gerald about her past.

Gerald's father flips through the pictures. "I'll frame them and put them up in my apartment."

The car stops at a red light and Gerald's father slides a picture of Valerie over to him. "She has such a pretty smile." He watches his son for a few moments. "What's wrong, Gerald?"

Gerald shrugs. "Nothing."

"Then why can't you look at the picture of Valerie?"

Gerald is quiet for a long time. He realizes he has to tell his father something. "I didn't want to talk about it right now, but Val and I broke up."

Gerald's father shakes his head. "Sorry about that. What happened?"

"Something from her past came up."

"The past—it can be worked out, right?"

"This can't be worked out," Gerald says adamantly.

"I had a past and you deal with me."

Gerald shakes his head. "This is different."

"If you say so," his father says with a sigh.

Gerald sees the disapproving look on his face. "I know what you're thinking. In your case, dad, things you did happened a long time ago. You're a different person now."

Gerald's father is quiet for a few moments. He won't tell Gerald that he knows Valerie's secret.

"Isn't she a different person now?"

"Dad, I can't trust her and I don't think she ever loved me."

They pull up to the restaurant. Gerald's father gets out of the car as he says, "People do different things to hurt you, but forgiveness is always the same." Gerald looks thoughtfully at his father as they walk inside.

Valerie

After she leaves Gerald's house, Valerie stays in her car in the drugstore parking lot and cries her heart out. A woman walks by and knocks on the car window. "Are you okay?" she calls out.

Valerie rolls down the window. "Yes, I'm okay, thanks."

"Well, you know, life can be like lemons. But adding sugar makes it lemonade," the woman says. Valerie tries to smile and nods as the woman walks to her car, gets in and drives off. Valerie still can't end her tears. She starts crying again, but is now at least finally able to drive to her apartment.

Valerie wakes up the next morning with a pounding headache. She heads to a nearby Starbucks for coffee. She's grateful that she doesn't have to work today—it's her day off—she certainly wouldn't want the store manager to see her like this. Once back in her apartment, Valerie immediately snatches several self-help books from the bookshelf and begins flipping through them. Some books deal with romantic relationships, others with emotional pain after someone dies. But none of the books that usually give her comfort, give any comfort now. She throws the books to the floor, flops onto the sofa and cries. It's too painful to contemplate her life without Gerald in it.

The next day Valerie calls in sick and spends the next several days staying in bed and watching various self-help gurus on TV. She barely nibbles on the sparse offerings of food in the refrigerator. One day after seeing a TV commercial featuring dancers twirling across stage, she remembers Marisa (her real name is Alicia), an old friend in the escort business. She wonders if Alicia would want to see her after all this time, but also remembers that Alicia was always supportive and that's what Valerie needs right now. She calls but there's no answer so she leaves a message saying that she's coming over and hopes Alicia will be home by the time she gets there.

Valerie's spirits lift as she nears the familiar red brick house at the end of a cul-de-sac. Rakes, shovels, and cans of blue paint sit near the front door. She nervously knocks on the door.

The door cracks open and Alicia stands there scowling, twisting strands of her long dark hair around her finger. She softens when she sees Valerie's bloodshot eyes and pale face. "You look horrible."

"I know," Valerie says.

Alicia opens the door all the way and Valerie goes inside. Valerie sniffs. "It smells like paint."

They step around pieces of a sectional couch, coffee table, and TV in the narrow hallway as they walk into the living room. "Yes, we painted two days ago. Excuse the mess," Alicia says pointing to the bright yellow walls. "Everyone is at my cousin's to help with a house repair."

Valerie looks relieved. "Good. Even though I would love to see them, I'm just not up to it today."

"Are you hungry?" Alicia asks as she walks toward the kitchen. Alicia looks over her shoulder. "Watch your step," she says they walk on a drop cloth and step over paint brushes on the floor.

"Not really, but I probably should eat something."

"How about I heat up some leftover enchiladas?"

Valerie smiles. "That sounds good, you know I love your cooking. Have you seen any good ballets?"

Alicia nods as she places the skillet on top of the stove and turns it on. "I just saw a Russian dance troupe at Georgia Tech. They were great. I haven't been to dance class in a while; hopefully, I can start again next week. So, what's up with you?"

Valerie sighs. "Well, to make a long story short: I had a boyfriend, the relationship became serious, and then I told him that I used to be a prostitute." She wipes tears from her eyes. "Now he hates me."

"I'm sorry, Valerie." Alicia leaves and comes back with a box of tissues and hands it to Valerie. "Why did you tell him anyway?"

"I wanted to be honest."

Alicia shakes her head. "That *never* works."

"I had to. But enough about this. I need to hear something good. What's going on with you?"

"We're back in the restaurant business!" Alicia says.

Valerie says, "I know! I heard about it. That's great!"

Alicia throws her fists in the air. "You can't hold our family down for long."

Valerie high fives Alicia. "That's the truth! And Atlanta misses the best Cuban restaurant in town."

"Tony was such a bastard," Alicia says with a sneer.

Valerie blows her nose. "I'm sorry that you had to go through this."

"But now Tony has to pay up and we get to keep the restaurant."

"And you can stop seeing Tony and his jerk friends."

"No money yet," Alicia says. "There's one last court date in three months. I'm still "Marisa" and not quite out of the business, damn it."

Valerie nods. "You don't have much longer. FYI, Tony was also my boyfriend's former business partner."

"No way!"

Valerie slowly nods her head.

Alicia says, "You told your boyfriend about Tony?"

Valerie nods.

Alicia pats her on the back. "Girl, that's even worse than telling him everything. You shouldn't have told him *everything*, everything."

"I got sick and tired of constantly looking over my shoulder every time we went out, scared if a former client would recognize me. A big secret is a big burden."

"Which is why I wouldn't have a man while I'm in the business," Alicia says. "Too much trouble. So, where are you working?"

"At Trendz boutique in midtown. I really like it."

"You know it was messed up how you did me," Alicia says as she turns the enchiladas in the pan. They're sizzling and the delicious aroma permeates the kitchen. "Being told on voicemail that you quit the business and disconnecting your number—damn Valerie, I thought we were close."

"We are close. I'm sorry but I needed to get away from anyone in the business since I was making a change. Please understand and don't be mad."

"I was mad when I got your message today," Alicia says as she gets two plates, silverware and napkins and sets them on the table. "I planned on cursing you out when I saw you but I couldn't. You always have been a good friend. And you were the only sane escort I knew that wasn't on drugs or totally crazy. Sorry I hooked you up with Tony. I don't think your man will ever forgive that."

Valerie shrugs. "It's not your fault. I'm sorry for running off. We'll stay in touch from now on."

They hug each other tightly until Alicia pulls back. "Okay, okay. Don't make me cry. C'mon let's eat."

Valerie rubs her eyes and sits at the table. "I don't want to cry either. I'm all out of tears."

They're eating and Alicia is telling a story about how she fell in dance class in front of a cute male dancer. "He tried catching me, but he fell, too. I had no grace whatsoever. I was clumsy like a giraffe on skis. No way was he going to find me attractive after that." They both laugh. At that moment, Ernesto and his son come into the kitchen.

Valerie smiles, jumps up and hugs them both. "I missed you two!" The men respond in rapid Spanish and embrace Valerie as if she's a member of the family.

Valerie feels much better being around people who care about her. It helps, if only temporarily to relieve the relentless pain she feels having lost the only man she ever loved.

Chapter 35
CHANGES

Gerald

Christy leans close to the bathroom mirror as she puts on bright red lipstick. Then she smoothes down her dark hair and turns around to look at herself from the back. "You know, since I'm meeting some clients at the club at Chops, let's just have dinner there when I'm done."

Gerald stands in the doorway to the bathroom admiring her long legs in a tight black leather skirt. "Last week you said you would go to the dinner movie theater."

Christy pulls earrings out of her weekend bag sitting on the counter. He steps behind her as she puts them on. She stares at him in the mirror. "My dearrr...you know I don't really do movies. When did you start liking movies for dates? You're acting well...a little strange."

Gerald smirks. "I'm *not* strange. And besides, change is a good thing. Let's do something different. We always go to five-star restaurants."

She bats her eyelashes at him as innocently as Bambi. "Sorry, I didn't mean it like that. Don't be mad. I just don't do movies. Please, can we eat at

Chops? I have on an outfit too fabulous to waste on a movie. And I'm dying to eat a good steak."

Gerald is irritated. He nods. "Okay, my wine and dine woman, what time?"

She zips up her bag, steps out the bathroom into Gerald's office to put on her mink fur coat lying on his couch. "Eight o'clock. See you then."

Gerald leans in to kiss her on the lips but Christy turns her head and kisses the air above his cheek so her lipstick won't smudge, picks up her briefcase and leaves. Gerald shakes his head.

Gerald had brooded over Valerie for more than a month before he started seeing Christy. He had been running an errand and a young couple coming out of a jewelry store walked by him talking about the bride-to-be's engagement ring. He remembered the vision his father gave him about marrying Christy. Gerald wonders why he wasted time with Valerie, especially considering that as time went by, his father's visions proved to be accurate. He wanted to get back on track to what it should have been to begin with. When he called Christy she practically jumped through the phone with anticipation.

But after a couple of months, Gerald realizes everything with Christy is the same as it always had been. She likes to eat out at the best restaurants and go to exclusive V.I.P. events in town. Home cooked meals are just not her thing, even if Gerald offers to cook. Christy likes to be seen. Business and networking are her forte. She's very helpful to Gerald in business and introduces him to good contacts. Sometimes it feels like she's more a business partner than a girlfriend.

At dinner Gerald is in a bad mood since he didn't want to go in the first place, so Christy is extra charming and tells funny stories to put him in a better mood. They're laughing at something she says and Christy grabs his hand. It flashes in Gerald's mind that it's just like what he saw in his father's vision, except there is no ring and he doesn't want to propose. He feels like an actor who forgot his lines. What he's supposed to say, to be doing—he's nowhere near what is in the script.

After dinner they go back to Gerald's house and he heads into his office.

Gerald looks in a file cabinet as Christy sits on the side of the desk. "I'm so glad you have an office at home. I need to set up an area in one of your extra bedrooms so I can work."

He closes the cabinet, puts papers on his desk, scribbles something on a post-it note and sticks it on the stack of papers. "You should relax when you come here. I'm glad that I don't work like I used to. I have more time to volunteer and spend time with my father."

"You really enjoy working at the shelter."

Gerald cuts off the light. They leave the office and head to the bedroom. "I keep asking you to come with me. Lee is a wonderful woman and you'll learn a lot from the homeless residents."

"I prefer my charity work," Christy says, sounding defensive. "You know I'm head of the planning committee for the Women's Guild holiday fundraiser for needy children."

"I know," Gerald says. "Do you work directly with the kids?" He knows that her volunteering consists of hosting a black tie event at the Ritz Carlton in Buckhead and inviting company big-wigs to attend and write big checks.

Christy goes into the walk-in closet and takes off her clothes. "Occasionally, I see some kids at events."

"That's good," Gerald says without enthusiasm.

Christy changes into a green silk nightgown. "I was thinking about volunteering to work with recent college grads interested in learning about commercial insurance. It's a great way to recruit people to work for me. Why don't you set up a volunteer center for M.B.A. students to get publicity for your business and get some new clients?"

"I don't need any more business," Gerald says.

She looks surprised. "But you're always working on the next big deal."

Gerald hangs up his suit on a rack in the corner of the bedroom and changes into a robe hanging on the back of the door. "That was the old me. I've cut down on work to enjoy other things in life."

"I've never heard you talk this way before," Christy says. "Won't you get bored not being on top?"

Gerald frowns. "No. I've been doing this for a while now." He turns away from Christy.

She senses he's angry. "Sorry, I didn't realize this was so important to you."

She comes behind him and puts her arms around his chest and kisses the side of his face to distract him from being irritated. Gerald is unresponsive, so Christy walks in front of him and kisses his tight lips. He finally kisses her back and Christy slowly inches him toward the bed. He stops her.

"We need to talk," Gerald says softly.

Christy tilts her head to the side. "I know," she responds. "I already know that something isn't right."

"It's not you, it's me."

She laughs. "That's such a cliché."

"I didn't mean for it to come out like that. But it is me. You're the same as you've always been. I'm the one who's different. It's my fault."

Christy turns toward him. "I just don't understand this new you. Maybe I can try harder to make it work."

"No. I don't think we should see each other anymore," Gerald says with sadness in his voice.

Christy expected him to say this. She kisses him and without saying anything else, puts her clothes on, looks at him one last time, then leaves.

Gerald awakes the next morning refreshed. Christy was good for the man he was back then, but not for the man he is now. And, what's missing is love. What's missing is Valerie. He has been so foolish to think he could live without her. He's certain about what he needs to do.

Valerie

Valerie got back from Alicia's house and jumps right into work. Despite making stupid mistakes, her boss is very understanding especially since the boutique is doing a big, tropical themed fashion show. Everyone at work, except Valerie, is excited about showcasing summer fashions in the middle of winter, as if to make the cold weather magically disappear. Somehow Valerie gets through putting together the outfits for the models and organizing the show, but she's happy when it's over. Valerie's not the same anymore and she doesn't go to the shelter for fear of running into Gerald. It's especially hard since she passes Open Door every day on her way to work. She misses doing all the things she used to do. And above all, she misses Gerald. It's hard to move on and release the fog from her mind.

Valerie sits on the couch in her living room staring into space. Then she gets up to make sure the bathroom is clean even though she scrubbed it more than an hour ago. She double-checks the bedroom, a scented candle is lit.

The phone rings and a man says, "Hi, Sienna. My meeting ran late. Can I still come by?"

"Sure, no problem," Valerie says to the man on the other end of the phone.

"Good. I didn't want you to think I wasn't showing up. I didn't think I'd find your ads again after they'd been gone for so long."

"Well, I'm back."

She hangs up. Valerie feels something scratchy on her back and pulls a price tag off that's inside her clothes. She looks at the lingerie she has on. Too bad she had thrown her "work clothes" away but she didn't think she would ever be working again. Valerie has been drawn back to the business—loneliness and hopelessness are the culprits. The business is familiar. And the way things are going at the boutique Valerie doesn't know if she can work there anymore. She's even thinking about quitting if they don't fire her first.

There's a knock on the door. Valerie lets out a big sigh, walks to the door and opens it.

He steps inside, grinning from ear to ear like it's his birthday and she's his gift. "Hey, baby. You still look good." He smiles and lustfully scans her body with his eyes.

"Thanks." She looks at…at—she thinks his name is Jeff—his bald head and big belly bulging out over the waist of his tailored pants. Unfortunately, he looks the same as before.

Valerie motions to the bedroom as Jeff hands her an envelope with money.

She puts the money on the nightstand. He takes off his jacket and shirt, then his pants. Her mind becomes numb.

"So, how are you?" he asks.

"Right back where I started," Valerie says, as they both climb into bed.

Chapter 36
VALERIE'S MISTAKE

The next morning, when Valerie walks out of her bedroom she notices his watch on her nightstand. Valerie frowns. She remembers seeing Jeff take it off and she doesn't want to see him again to give it back. She puts the watch inside the drawer and sends him a text message asking him for his address so she can mail it to him. Then Valerie goes into the kitchen to make some tea. There's a knock on the door. For a moment she thinks it might be Jeff coming back to retrieve his watch.

Valerie opens the door to see Gerald standing there.

"We need to talk," he says.

He walks in and looks at her intensely, his hazel eyes boring straight into her. Valerie blinks several times. He looks thinner than what she remembered. Her heart beats so fast that she gets dizzy.

He leads her into the living room and both sit on opposite ends of the couch.

Valerie hangs her head low. "I'm sorry for not telling you the truth sooner."

Gerald shakes his head. "Let me start off by saying that I'm sorry for how I reacted. You told me the truth when you didn't have to."

She looks at him in surprise.

"It was a shock, I admit. It hurt my ego. No man wants to think of the woman he's involved with sleeping with lots of men. And with all that, it's still no excuse for what I said to you. I forgive you."

Valerie bursts into tears.

Gerald takes her in his arms and cradles her like a baby. "Don't cry. Shh, I promise you, it's all in the past."

Valerie can't help but cry. Just hours ago she had gotten into bed with Jeff and as soon as he stroked her breasts she felt dirty. She immediately jumped up and ran into the bathroom. Through the closed bathroom door, she told him to leave, not call anymore, and that she was sorry. Valerie waited until she heard him leave the apartment and when she came out, she went straight to the computer and deleted all her escort ads before taking a shower. And now she's crying tears of happiness and relief.

"Feel better now?" Gerald asks.

Valerie sniffles. "I'm okay."

Gerald wipes the wetness from her cheeks. "You know, one of the things I thought about was how you stayed on me to work things out with my father. It was hard to do. You showed me that forgiveness is the key to everything. And, there's no way I couldn't forgive you when I forgave him. Please forgive me."

Valerie stops crying and lifts her head. "I forgive you."

He smiles. "I love you, Val."

Valerie smiles back. "I love you, too."

Gerald gets up from the couch and reaches into his pocket to pull out a beautiful heart shaped diamond engagement ring. "Will you marry me?"

Valerie stares at the ring, then at Gerald. She screams. "Of course I'll marry you!" He takes her trembling hand and puts the ring on her finger.

They kiss and hold each other and continue kissing.

"Do you have any wine?" Gerald asks. "We need to celebrate."

Gerald goes into the kitchen and sees a big, beautiful bouquet of exotic flowers on the kitchen's round beige table.

Valerie comes into the kitchen. "Where did you get these flowers?" he asks.

"Oh, they were left over from a fashion show the boutique had the other day. Why?"

He chuckles and pours them both some wine as he says, "I saw these flowers in my dream that night when you suspected I was getting visions from my father."

She smiles. "These same ones. Really?"

"Yes."

Valerie asks, "So you knew you were going to ask me to marry you?"

Gerald remembers the first vision his father gave him and how he misunderstood it to mean that he was marrying Christy. "Yes and no. In an earlier vision my father showed me with the ring I just gave you. I didn't know I would be proposing to you until a few days ago."

She shakes her head. "It's amazing how all your father's visions come true."

Gerald raises his glass. "To my father's visions and getting married."

"And to forgiveness," Valerie says.

"Yes," Gerald says. "Forgiveness is the key to everything."

Over the next several days Valerie and Gerald pick a wedding date and tell friends and family. Gerald asks his father to be his best man and the old man accepts. Seeing the happiness on Gerald's father's face makes Valerie think of her mother. She would love for her mother to be a part of the wedding, but she has no idea where she is. Valerie decides to drive by her old neighborhood where she grew up to see if anyone has seen her. Sometimes when her mom got disoriented she would come back to the house she grew up in even though she didn't live there anymore. The house had been sold years earlier.

Valerie stops by several neighbor's homes and they tell her that they saw her mom up by the creek a few days ago. This was typical of her mother. Valerie parks on the side of the street and walks down the hill that leads to the creek. She remembers the many times she would run and play around here when her mom would be gone for days. There's a flat tire, empty soft drink cans, and other trash floating in the creek, much more trash than she remembered.

Valerie walks further down the side of the creek and calls out, "Mom, Mom!"

She doesn't see her. "Mom, are you here? It's Valerie!"

A tree branch snaps on the other side of the creek and falls on the ground. Valerie quickly walks across the creek in the direction of the tree. She sees her mother ducking behind the tree.

"Mom, are you okay? Come out from behind there."

Her mother steps from behind the tree. She has on a thick black wool coat. "Hi."

Valerie carefully looks at her mother. She doesn't appear disoriented. "How have you been?"

"I'm okay. I guess. I'm okay."

"Well let's get out of here," Valerie says. "Want some coffee?"

Her mother looks at the cloud of cold mist coming from Valerie's mouth as she speaks. She shudders and digs her hands deep into her pockets. "Yes, that would be nice."

They drive to a Starbucks up the street and sit at a table, sipping hot coffee.

Valerie looks closely at her mother. She's small with the slight figure she always had, and large green eyes that seem to take up most of her heart-shaped face. She has on a clean wool sweater and jeans, is sitting still and not jumping all over the place.

"Mom, why were you hiding? You look like you're taking your meds, right?"

Her mother nods and slowly stirs her coffee.

"I'm glad. I worry about you. You look good."

What Valerie really means is that she looks normal, lucid, not disheveled. "Where have you been all this time?"

"I was down at Grady Hospital for a bit. After I left there I stayed on the streets for a few months. Now, I'm staying with a friend."

"Mom, you can always stay with me. I don't want you on the streets. That's dangerous."

"I know why you're looking for me."

Valerie is surprised. "How did you find out?"

Her mother hangs her head down, smoothing loose hair back into her long ponytail. "I know you figured out what I did. I can't pay you back."

Valerie is confused until it hits her that her mom is referring to the money she took from her purse the day in the apartment after she had seen her client.

"Sorry I stole the money," her mother says sheepishly.

"That's in the past, mom. Apology accepted but that's not why I was looking for you."

"Really? Then, why?"

Valerie smiles broadly. "I have great news, I'm getting married!"

Her mother's eyes widen. "That's wonderful. Who is the lucky man?"

"His name is Gerald. I want you to meet him."

Her mom coughs and looks away. "You want me to meet him? That's hard to believe. I don't want to embarrass you."

"I told him all about you, mom, and he wants to meet you."

"And he's okay with...with...my problems?"

Valerie sips some coffee. "Mom, look at me." She looks at Valerie. "Gerald loves me and wants you to be a part of my life, both of our lives. All I ever wanted was for us to have a normal relationship."

Her mom sees the sincerity of Valerie's words in her eyes. "He sounds like a good man. Maybe I can meet him if I can get myself together so I won't make you look bad."

Valerie nods and smiles. "Gerald is a good man. Taking your medication will help you get yourself together. How long have you been taking them this time?"

Valerie's mom looks irritated. "Two weeks."

"That's good. But you need to stay on them."

Her mother says tightly, "I don't like medication. I won't take it."

"Mom, please don't start this all over again. The best thing for you is to take the meds. You're stable that way. Like right now, you're on them and you're behaving normally."

"You don't know what it's like. I hate the meds!" her mother shouts.

Valerie scowls. "Mom, I hate you being this way. It wasn't supposed to be this way!" She quiets downs after a few people look over at their table. "Do you know how difficult it was growing up? I had to take care of you instead of the other way around. So many times I've worried where you've been, if you've been hurt or worse, dead."

Valerie's mother sadly stares into her coffee cup, close to tears. "I'm sorry, Valerie. I didn't mean to ruin your life. I'm really sorry. But when I take that stuff I'm in a fog, it's like my mind is stuffed with rags. I'm a zombie. I just want to have my mind right. You have no idea how it is. Please forgive me." She bursts into tears.

"Mom, please don't cry," Valerie says, on the verge of tears herself. "I'll always be there for you. I'll try harder to deal with your mental illness, to understand it from your point of view. I'll help you find some medication that won't affect you so badly. Maybe we can find an herbal remedy that works for you and won't have bad side effects. We can do this together. Will you promise to try?"

Valerie's mother nods. "I promise. I don't want to be a burden. I want you to be happy with your fiancé and I want to be the right kind of mother for once."

Valerie reaches for her mother's hand and holds it tightly. "That's all I ever wanted."

Valerie remembers the vision the old man gave her months ago. It showed her sitting with her mother over coffee just like they are now. The vision had come true. *All his visions had come true* for Gerald and for her. Valerie could never have imagined that she and her mother would be talking to each other the way they are now.

* * *

On the other side of town, Chantal has now been trying for weeks to find the old man, but to no avail. She paces back and forth in her dingy motel room. Hunger punches knots in the bottom of her stomach and grumbles loudly. The sound agitates Chantal. When it continues she remembers that she hasn't eaten in two days.

There's a knock on the door and Chantal opens it to find her mother standing outside. Lee looks worried when she sees how thin Chantal looks. "You look terrible. Why haven't you answered the phone?" she asks her daughter.

Chantal sighs. "I'm fine mother, I've just been busy," she says as her mother comes inside.

"Busy doing what? You've lost so much weight. Have you seen a dcctor?"

"I don't need a doctor. I'm just getting over a cold," Chantal answers. "Mother, I'm planning to go back to France," she says abruptly.

Lee looks shocked. "Oh," she says and pauses a few moments. "I thought you were staying here for good. When are you leaving?"

"Soon, very soon," Chantal replies. "I'd rather be alone right now."

"I'll leave. You'll call me later?" Lee asks.

"Sure."

Lee looks at her daughter as she leaves. She has a strong feeling that Chantal will leave town without saying goodbye, and there's nothing she can do about it. Lee silently prays for Chantal as she drives away.

After her mother leaves Chantal looks at herself in the mirror—her face is drawn and thin. No wonder her mother said she looked bad. She knows she must take care of herself, but her desperation has turned to despair—she's convinced the old man, her salvation, her last shred of hope, will never be fcund.

Chapter 37
NEW LIFE

The big, bearded man looks over his shoulder several times as he fumbles with a pick at the lock of the door. Earlier, he saw the old man leave the apartment. His fingers move precisely while jimmying the lock. With a loud click he finally coaxes the door open. He has a twisted grin of satisfaction on his face. He had followed the old man home the day that Chantal had talked to him and had been in the apartment before this evening, but every time he had tried to get the old man, people were around. But now all he has to do is wait for the old man to come back home, then revenge for his brother will finally happen.

Gerald and Valerie drop Gerald's father off at the apartment that night after they've all been to dinner together. Gerald's father puts his key in the lock and without turning the key the door opens. He frowns as he puts down the green suitcase which he still carries with him. He turns on the light in the living room. He walks around the living room and bedroom as he phones Gerald.

The call goes straight to voicemail and he leaves an urgent message: "Someone broke in. Nothing is missing. I'm calling the police. Maybe it's time for me to move in with you."

Gerald's father hangs up and begins dialing the phone as he hears footsteps coming from the bathroom.

He drops the phone. "What the—!" He's staring in shock at Chantal.

"I didn't break in," she says, "but I saw the man who did earlier. He ran off when he saw me coming. I think it was the guy who attacked you at Open Door."

He glares at her. "Why are you here?"

"I need to talk to you," Chantal begs.

Gerald's father groans. "Hmm...you've been following me."

She strokes the scarf tied around her neck. "No. I was out earlier to get something to eat and saw Gerald and Valerie turning into the apartments at the traffic light."

He grunts. "Like I said, you followed me."

"No, not really."

"Whatever you call it, I don't like. You look sick. Go home and take care of yourself. Go."

Chantal wrings her hands and begins to shake. "Wait a minute, please. I need your help."

"I told you before I can't help you. I got my own problems."

"Please heal my face and I'll leave you alone."

She steps close to him and puts her cold, clammy hand on top of his. "Here take my hand like you did with Gerald. Use your power."

Gerald's father tries to pull away but Chantal won't let go. They pull back and forth in a tug of war. Her sunglasses slip off her face and fall to the floor.

"For the last time, it doesn't work that way!" he cries out as he steps away from her.

Chantal screams, "Use your power!"

She quickly reaches into her purse and pulls out a long, pointy, metal nail file and aims it at him. She walks toward him, shaking, the nail file in her hand. "You have to help me!"

The old man sees the wild look in Chantal's eyes, then looks toward the front door and makes a run for it. She chases him and grabs him roughly by the arm. The old man trips over a rug and they both crash to the floor. Chantal falls on top of him and he lands hard on his arm. "Ahh!" he yells as pain shoots up his arm.

They scuffle on the floor. Chantal grabs the front of his shirt and he kicks her away. She falls backward onto a small table and it falls over—books and a glass vase crash to the floor. The vase shatters. The old man pulls himself up on his elbow and scoots backwards on the floor as he tries to get away from her. Chantal gets up, slips on the broken shards of glass. Then steadies herself and jumps on top of him and plunges the nail file deeply into his neck. Blood immediately gushes out and down his shirt. Chantal is frozen, her hand still on the file as blood spills onto her hand. His eyes fixate on her. His wrinkles begin to glow and vibrate. She opens her mouth in a soundless gasp and reaches up with her other hand to touch the wrinkles on his cheek. Blood trickles from the corner of his mouth onto her hand. Chantal pulls her hand away. Gerald's father closes his eyes and his head falls back on the floor with a thud. It's hard to breathe. He tastes blood in his mouth. His throat is clogged and throbs in pain. Memories fill his head, fighting with the man—his friend from long ago.

The man is on the floor next to a broken coffee table. His eye is red and his knuckles are bleeding. They're in the man's living room. Gerald's father is bloody. He sways a little, stumbling next to him. Gerald's father can't feel his nose. He touches it, blood covers his hand. His nose leans a little to the right. It's broken.

Mark—he remembers clearly now, that's his friend's name, broke his nose.

He says to Mark, "Where's my two thousand dollars?!"

He feels his mouth fill with blood and spits it on the floor. He and Mark drank and gambled together all the time. This time Mark owed him money.

Mark tries to stand up but falls back down. "I don't have it right now." His voice is garbled.

He kicks Mark hard in the ribs. "Liar! I know the money is here!"

Mark cries out in pain and grabs his chest. "Please...I'm not...lying. Stop Na-" He can hardly speak.

He leans over Mark and angrily spits blood in his face.

Gerald's father opens his eyes. They droop down and almost close again. What did Mark start to say? Nate? His thoughts drift in and out. He thinks, *Finally...know. Nate. Nathaniel...my name.* He smiles. Chantal watches him closely. He looks relieved and peaceful. Very peaceful.

His breathing slows down to short, shallow bursts. Chantal can tell he's slipping away. She pulls her hand away from the file as the last breath leaves his body. The air feels thick and warm around her. Aloud she whispers, "Oh,

God, what did I do?" She starts crying as she stares in horror at his lifeless body on the floor, the smile still on his face. Chantal strokes his arm as if he's listening. "I didn't mean to kill you. I just wanted you to make me pretty." His past floats in the heavy air.

Mark pleads. "No, no…"

Nathaniel puts his hands around Mark's neck and squeezes hard. He can feel his neck pulse beneath his fingertips. Mark grabs frantically at his hands but can't pry them off. Mark thrashes around for about a minute and then gradually stops moving. Nathaniel releases Mark's neck and sees indentations of his fingers on his neck. He stares blankly at his friend. Nathaniel puts his head in his hands, then looks back up. He says, "I…didn't mean to kill you. I just wanted my money." Then he sees something across the room.

The wrinkles on the old man's face are still moving. Chantal touches his face and grabs his hands. She rips the scarf from around her head and frantically touches the left side of her face. "Please…please." But the burns are still there and she cries harder.

Chantal sees something across the room. It's the green suitcase. Red and white fabrics sticking out of the sides are glowing. She walks over to it. She opens the suitcase slowly as if it's a treasure chest filled with gold. The air becomes heavy again with Nathaniel's memories.

He sees a green suitcase across the room in the corner near a bookcase. He wonders if his money is in it. Nathaniel stumbles to the suitcase and opens it up. All that's inside is some red and white fabric. He wonders where else to look for the money. Nathaniel feels lightheaded and sits down next to the suitcase. The fabrics begin to glow. Nathaniel's eyes widen in surprise and his thoughts begin to...

Chantal looks inside the green suitcase. There's a crumpled yellow shirt and a pair of stained underwear briefs on top. She wrinkles her nose in distaste. "Yuck." She gingerly picks through the clothes throwing them on the floor. There's a lot of stuff in it: dried chili peppers, holey pants, a faded green shirt, Chanel red flame #69 lipstick—wait a minute, this is from my purse, how did that get in here? The lipstick sits on top of a white swimsuit that David bought her three years ago when on holiday in Monte Carlo—what the?!—she left that in France. She quickly digs deeper, her mind reeling. There's a pair of baby shoes set in bronze and a piece of construction paper with her tiny handprints in red and blue paint. Chantal gasps and a chill goes down her spine. Only her mom has these things. Something isn't right. How did these get here? She keeps pulling out things when she notices the floor is now piled with enough stuff to fill two huge trash bags. There is no possible way that all of that came from the suitcase.

Chantal reaches into it again. She sees glowing white fabric. She touches it—it's gauzy and fluffy like cotton balls. She sees glowing red fabric and touches it. She hears a sizzling sound before flames singe her fingertips. Chantal quickly snatches her hand away. "Ahh!" Then she sees her face reflected at the bottom of the suitcase floating in clouds and flames, except her entire face is burned, encompassed in thick scars. Chantal screams and touches her face, it's the same. She jumps back from the suitcase. Droplets of moisture float in the air and turn into condensation as if on a mirror. They form into a shape of the man with the green suitcase. He looks worried and sad. The wrinkles on his face are glowing and running down his face like streams of water. For an instant, his face changes into an image of Chantal's face. Her face is now filled with wrinkles just like his. "Oh my God!," Chantal screams. Then her face goes away and his face reappears again. Her mind, a river of thoughts, begins to trickle down to nothingness as her memory drains away. The next minute the wrinkles on his face are completely gone, floating from his feet toward her feet, traveling up her legs. Chantal futilely tries to brush them away. "No, no!" The wrinkles continue the journey up her chest, sliding up to her face.

He says, "I'm free. Now, it's your turn." Then the old man with the green suitcase disappears.

The next morning Gerald and Valerie rush to his father's apartment. They unlock the door and step inside. Gerald looks around. Everything is quiet except for the hum of the refrigerator in the kitchen. The curtains are closed. The apartment is clean and tidy as usual. Something seems different though.

"Dad! Dad!"

There's no sound as Gerald looks in the bedroom. The bed is neatly made up.

"It doesn't look like anyone broke in," Valerie says.

Gerald looks distraught. "Where could he be? I hate that we had the phone turned off last night when he called. We could have been here sooner."

"We're here now. Maybe he's at Open Door."

Gerald looks around the apartment and it hits him that the place isn't just quiet, it's empty as if no one lives there at all. The air feels still like inside a vacant apartment. He goes into the kitchen, opens the refrigerator. It's empty.

Gerald looks puzzled. "I bought him two bags of groceries a day ago, there's no food here."

Valerie looks inside the refrigerator. Gerald walks into the bedroom and she follows him. He opens his drawers and the closet. There are no clothes.

"That's strange. All his clothes are gone," Valerie says, a worried look on her face.

"What the hell is going on? Let's go to the shelter to see if he's there."

They leave the apartment and as Gerald locks the door he has a strong feeling that his father is gone for good. As they pull out of the parking lot they see the back of a woman wearing a thick coat and a scarf on her head walking down the street with a green suitcase.

Gerald says, "Is that Chantal?"

Valerie stares hard at the woman and then looks at Gerald. "That's her. But why is she carrying that green suitcase?"

Gerald pulls up along the sidewalk and rolls down the window. He yells out, "Chantal, where are you going?!"

Chantal stops and turns around. She doesn't have on her usual sunglasses. She peers at Gerald, the edges of her burned face peeking beneath the now disheveled scarf. Her face also now has deep wrinkles like that of someone very old. "You've got the wrong person. I don't know you."

Gerald and Valerie stare at her in shock as Chantal turns back around and keeps walking. The green suitcase gently swings in her hand. There's a long journey ahead and many places to go. Until she finds where she needs to go she will just keep walking with the green suitcase. She's not walking fast. She's not walking slow. She's just walking.